"How did you disable two

"Self-defense classes," Meg

"Ernie says you put both down without a weapon," Griff insisted. "I couldn't have. Not without an advantage. What advantage did you have?"

"The cash register. I slammed it over his head after I kicked him...well, you know where."

"And what was the other guy doing?"

"He waved his gun at me, but the big guy got up and knocked him over. It was a total accident but worked to my advantage."

Her knuckles were swollen and blue.

"You need something for that?"

"It's okay. I've suffered worse, believe—" She caught herself too late.

"It feels like there are things you need to tell me. How you can take down two men all alone. Or stop a man carrying a gun with only a knife."

"Self-defense classes." The lie was sounding weaker all the time.

"You can tell me anything. You know that, right?"

"I do. We're friends."

"Then why aren't you telling me?"

Reader Note

Piney Woods is a small community that I tweaked just for this story. I loved the name and I wanted to create the small-town atmosphere this book needed. This is my fifth installment of the Lookout Mountain Mysteries. I've loved writing the characters and creating the settings, whether coming up with a completely fictional town or adjusting a real one to suit the story. This particular tale is one of my favorites. I just love this heroine. I hope you'll love her, too!

PERIL IN PINEY WOODS

USA TODAY Bestselling Author

DEBRA WEBB

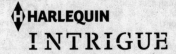

HARLEQUIN®
INTRIGUE™

Recycling programs
for this product may
not exist in your area.

ISBN-13: 978-1-335-59157-9

Peril in Piney Woods

Copyright © 2024 by Debra Webb

For questions and comments about the quality of this book, please contact us
at CustomerService@Harlequin.com.

TM and ® are trademarks of Harlequin Enterprises ULC.

Harlequin Enterprises ULC
22 Adelaide St. West, 41st Floor
Toronto, Ontario M5H 4E3, Canada
www.Harlequin.com

Printed in Lithuania

MIX
Paper | Supporting
responsible forestry
FSC® C021394

Debra Webb is the award-winning *USA TODAY* bestselling author of more than one hundred novels, including those in reader-favorite series Faces of Evil, the Colby Agency and Shades of Death. With more than four million books sold in numerous languages and countries, Debra has a love of storytelling that goes back to her childhood on a farm in Alabama. Visit Debra at debrawebb.com.

Books by Debra Webb

Harlequin Intrigue

Lookout Mountain Mysteries

Disappearance in Dread Hollow
Murder at Sunset Rock
A Place to Hide
Whispering Winds Widows
Peril in Piney Woods

A Winchester, Tennessee Thriller

In Self Defense
The Dark Woods
The Stranger Next Door
The Safest Lies
Witness Protection Widow
Before He Vanished
The Bone Room

Visit the Author Profile page at Harlequin.com.

CAST OF CHARACTERS

Megan "Meg" Lewis—Meg owns and operates Pampered Pets grooming. Her life is calm and simple until a robbery at a gas station across the street reveals a deep, dark secret that endangers her life.

Avery "Griff" Griffin—Griff gave up city life to return to the family farm where he rescues abandoned and abused animals. But can he rescue Meg when her past catches up to her?

Deputy Ernie Battles—Ernie and Griff have been friends their whole lives. Ernie is worried that something about Meg Lewis doesn't add up. What kind of dog groomer can take down men three times her size with nothing but her hands and her wits?

Angela "Angel" Hamilton—They call her the Angel of Death. Could this be Meg's true identity?

Deputy Director Arthur Wisting—Can Meg trust her former boss with the whole truth?

Sheriff Tara Norwood—A second-generation sheriff of Hamilton County, she knows this mountain and the people who live here better than anyone.

Chapter One

Pampered Paws
Piney Woods, Tennessee
Saturday, May 4, 10:00 p.m.

Megan Lewis was exhausted, but she smiled at her favorite pooch. "You got some nerve making me stay in the shop this late."

Raymond, her ten-year-old border collie, gazed up at her with those eyes that she could never resist. He lay on the floor next to the kennel door where the newest pet abandoned in front of her shop cowered in fear. Fortunately, incidents like this didn't happen very often—at least not at her shop. But when they did, she refused to let the animal down any more than it already had been.

She had no choice. Her heart wouldn't allow anything else.

The beagle that had been left on her doorstep early that morning wasn't a young animal. Meg suspected she was eight or ten. She'd found the poor baby at the front door before dawn. Couldn't be a local. Everyone in Piney Woods knew Meg lived upstairs. The only reason she hadn't heard the culprit's arrival or departure was because she'd been in the shower. But when she'd stepped out, Meg had certainly heard the animal's howl. Beagles had a distinct yodel-like sound.

Unlike most animals abandoned on the sides of roads or at vet clinics or even businesses like this one, there had been a note attached to the beagle's collar. The owner had explained that Pepper was not doing well, and the owner had no money to take care of her. She or he hoped that the owner of such a charming and caring place would be able to give Pepper the love and help she needed.

Certainly, Meg would try.

Just after lunch, Lonnie Howell, the local vet, had stopped in for a look. He would need to do more testing, but he suspected a heart issue. Meg was to drop Pepper at his clinic on Monday for the necessary testing and a more accurate diagnosis. Lonnie hadn't made any promises, but Meg knew him well enough to understand he would do whatever was necessary to help the animal whether there was money involved or not.

Meg crouched down and smiled at Pepper. "Don't worry, girl. We're going to take very good care of you, and once you're well enough, we'll see that you get a proper home. Just bear with me until then."

Pepper's sad eyes tugged at Meg's emotions. This career was definitely tougher in some ways than her former one. She gave Raymond a good scratch between the ears. She doubted he would be coming upstairs tonight. Raymond sensed when other animals were in an elevated state of stress. He stayed close when he felt his presence was needed.

"You're a good boy," Meg said before pushing to her feet.

She'd already locked up, but before going upstairs she made a final walk-through. The lobby was secure. The computer and drawers at the check-in counter were locked up. Since she wasn't open on Sundays, she used the day for a deep clean. She and one of her two employees—they alternated Sundays off—would spend the afternoon making the place shine. Cleanliness was important to Meg and to the animals. Folks trusted her with their beloved pets, and she wasn't about to let them down.

The kennels were all secure. Only three dogs and one cat were staying overnight. Pampered Paws was primarily a grooming service, but they did some boarding too—like the four presently registered for the weekend. No matter that Piney Woods was a small town, Meg actually had five customers whose dogs were on a weekly day care plan. The owners worked long days in the city of Chattanooga and had no one to look after their pets. Meg's shop was the first in Piney Woods to offer the service, and it had gone over far better than she'd anticipated.

In the beginning Meg hadn't expected to take on any extra services beyond grooming. She'd arrived in Piney Woods after having already purchased the small two-story building on the main street that cut through the center of the little town. After exiting her former career in a hasty manner, she'd decided her only other marketable skill had been with pets—mostly dogs. She'd grown up on a farm with lots of animals and no shortage of dogs. Her father, too, had taken in every stray that came along. Meg had shown a real knack with the lost animals. Her father had called her the dog whisperer. The term was a bit exaggerated, but she'd never met a dog—or any animal really—she couldn't get along with. They bonded quickly and easily. God knew she'd had all kinds of dogs and numerous cats throughout her life—particularly growing up on the farm, which made her well acquainted with the art of grooming. Seemed like the perfect fallback plan after her first choice fell apart.

She checked the back door and then headed upstairs to a studio apartment the former owner had used as a rental for extra income. The place was perfect for Meg. She didn't need much space. Just the basics. She unlocked the door and went inside, relocking it behind her. Crime in Piney Woods was basically nonexistent, but old habits died hard. Having a locked door between her and the rest of the world was the only way she could sleep—that and the one weapon she kept on her person at all times. No matter that in Tennessee it wasn't uncommon to see folks carrying a gun or knife, Meg preferred the element of surprise, which meant keeping hers carefully concealed.

Certainly, life was different here, but she liked it. On the farm in Bakersfield, California, where she'd grown up, she had learned to appreciate solitude. Not so much as a kid but certainly as an adult whenever she'd visited. The family farm hadn't been one of the massive multimillion dollar operations. Just a small vineyard and endless acres of fruit trees that had at one time provided a decent living to their little family.

Her heart squeezed at the memory of running

through the orchards with at least one dog on her heels and her father grinning at her for once again escaping the house when her mother had grounded her. She'd sneaked out so many times before age twelve that her mother had insisted she was going to be like Dorothy in *The Wizard of Oz*. One day she was just going to disappear, and no one would know where she'd gone. Her mother had warned that there might not be a yellow brick road to guide her to where she needed to go, much less to a wizard who could get her back home. Meg shook her head. She had loved that movie as a kid. She'd learned every line by heart and often played out the part of Dorothy, complete with running away. Not that she ever went very far or intended to stay gone. Looking back, Meg could only think that it was a good thing she'd been an only child. She wasn't sure her parents could have survived two like her.

Funny how her mother, may she rest in peace, had been more right about her daughter disappearing than she could possibly have known. Disappearing had become her job…

You can never go back.

Meg turned off the thought and flipped on the lights. That had been another time, another life.

She banished the memories. This was her life now. No point looking back.

She crossed the room and stared out the front window at the deserted street below. Piney Woods was the quintessential small town. One main thoroughfare, Pine Boulevard, which was really just a two-lane street with vintage shops lining the more "downtown" portion. Upon entering Piney Woods proper, there was a full-service gas station and convenience store just before reaching the sidewalks and vintage shops of the old downtown strip. Meg's place was the first shop on the left. A two-story brick building with a canopied entrance and meager parking out front. The parking slots along the boulevard were few and first come, first served.

The downstairs portion of her shop had long ago been tiled with a commercial grade product which made for the perfect flooring for a pet grooming service. She'd had some substantial plumbing upgrades completed, along with the framing up of separate spaces for kennels. Also lucky for her, since her shop was the first in the row on this side of the boulevard, she had a good-sized area in the back that could be a patio or extended parking. Instead, it had become a pet playground and had only two extra parking spots— one for her and for whichever of her two employees was on duty. Just over a year later, it turned out to be the right decision since five of her favorite clients had asked for pet-sitting services.

Another perk of her shop's location was the fact that she could see everyone who drove into town if she wanted to stand at the window and watch. There was a single main street that led into Piney Woods, and it dead-ended at the cliffs that overlooked the city of Chattanooga and the valley below. There were lots of little side roads in and around Piney Woods, but none led directly in or out of town. It was either come back out along Pine Boulevard or go over the cliffs at the other end or down the mountain along rugged trails on the two remaining sides. It was the perfect setup for someone who needed to meld into the background while monitoring the comings and goings around her.

Meg picked up the binoculars she kept on the deep windowsill. She eased onto it and used her binoculars to scan the street. The street lamps allowed her to see the sidewalks and any pedestrians who might be out and about. Folks who lived in Piney Woods were in for the night. She smiled. It wasn't like there was anything to do at this hour anyway.

The shops along the boulevard were closed. Most had dim exterior lighting. Some left a single low wattage light on inside as well. No one on the mountain wanted bright lights obscuring the view of the stars. The diner, the post office, a local pharmacy, a tiny bookstore and a small organic market were on the side of the boulevard opposite Pampered Paws. Another reason Meg had chosen this spot. At the time of her purchase, one year ago, the bookstore had been just a vacant shop. But it was on the wrong side of this little main thoroughfare for her use. She preferred being on the side with the small urgent care and the vintage furniture store.

Meg had wanted to be able to see folks coming in and out of the diner and those other more often visited shops by the folks passing through. She had made it a point to know the backgrounds of as many of the locals as possible—not that there were many. Keeping tabs on any new faces was important. Made life more comfortable for Meg.

She shifted her attention to the right, to the part of Pine Boulevard that transitioned into a county road where the Gas and Go, the gas station and convenience store combo—another key operation to keep an eye on—was lit up like the beacon of a lighthouse reaching out to anyone wandering in the dark. It was the only all-night gas and food service available for several miles. Further along that same county road was the fire station and a Hamilton County sheriff's substation. The bigger stores and supermarkets were a half hour or more away. Apparently, this was the way the citizens of Piney Woods liked it, because they had kept out all big business operations that showed interest in the area.

Another reason Meg had chosen this little town. Made her life all the easier.

She hoped things stayed the way they were.

Did anything? Ever?

Meg dismissed the troubling idea and zoomed in on the one vehicle parked at the Gas and Go.

Dark blue or black truck. Dented tailgate. Georgia license plate.

No surprise—they were very close to the Tennessee-Georgia line.

Jennifer O'Neal was on duty. Alone. The Gas and Go always had two employees on duty except for the late shift. Meg rolled her eyes. Sure, there might be less business at this hour, but it was prime time for trouble. Worse, the girl had just turned twenty-one. She was as thin and elfin as Tinker Bell.

"You should look for a better job, Jennifer," she muttered.

Meg zoomed in on the young woman behind the counter. Jennifer's eyes were wide with something like fear…her mouth opened slightly as if preparing to scream. *What the hell?* Meg's heart thumped as she zoomed back out far enough to take in the man who now stood at the counter.

Gun.

The gun in his hand sent Meg's heart into her throat. She put aside the binoculars, grabbed her cell and headed for the stairs in a dead run.

By the time she reached the back door downstairs, she had Deputy Sheriff Ernie Battles on the line. "Ernie, this is Meg. There's a—" Meg bit her tongue to hold back the code "—what looks like a robbery happening at the Gas and Go. The perp is armed with a handgun."

"On my way," Ernie said quickly, then he swore. "I'm maybe ten minutes out."

The rumble of the cruiser's engine roared over the line as he obviously rammed the accelerator.

"Should I call 911?" Meg had to do something. She couldn't just stand here.

"They won't get there any faster but go ahead. I need to drive."

The call ended.

Meg's gut clenched hard, and drawing in a breath was nearly impossible as she unlocked the back door and slipped out. As she moved through the darkness to the front corner of her shop, she called 911. She provided the necessary info, then hung up and shut off the ringer of her phone. The operators and dispatchers preferred to keep a caller on the line or to call back under certain circumstances. Meg didn't have the time for additional conversation, and she certainly didn't want her phone ringing or vibrating in the next few minutes.

She flattened against the building, held perfectly still and watched the movements of the two inside the Gas and Go. The guy with the gun was shouting. Jennifer was cowering in fear.

Ten minutes. Another twist to her gut at the idea that Jennifer did not have ten minutes.

Meg glanced both ways. The street remained empty.

This guy would be long gone, and Jennifer could be dead in ten minutes.

Meg swore. Then she sprinted across the street.

She hunkered down as she reached the perimeter of the well-lit parking lot. The truck—obviously the one belonging to the man with the gun—shielded her to some extent from view.

Keep going.

Meg moved closer.

Though she no longer carried a gun on her person, she did keep a sheathed knife at the small of her back. It was easier to conceal than a handgun. She reached for it now. Small, lightweight. Made for survival.

On the driver's side, since it was shielded from view, she stabbed both tires, twisted and dragged the blade to ensure the job was done. Stabbing through the sidewalls of tires wasn't an easy task but her knife was very sharp and it wasn't her first time. Plus, she was strong. She may have left her former career, but she hadn't walked away from staying fit and prepared. It was too essential to her survival.

With that done, she eased to the front fender to get an update on what was happening inside.

The perp had pulled Jennifer from behind the counter and was dragging her toward the short corridor that led into the back storage area of the building. Meg had only been back there once. She'd come over for paper towels, and Jennifer had been too busy to leave the counter to go into the back for more since she hadn't had a chance to restock that night. Meg had a general idea of the layout. There was a back door. The guy could do whatever he had in mind and then slip out the rear of the building.

Dread swelled in Meg's chest.

There was only one reason for him to take Jennifer into the back…before taking off with whatever cash had been in the register. He either wanted to play with her, or he intended to kill her…maybe both.

Deputy Battles absolutely would not get here in time to stop either situation.

"Damn it," Meg muttered.

She tightened her grip on the knife and lunged toward the entrance. With her free hand, she grabbed the door handle and held her breath. Opening it wouldn't be the problem. It was the door's closing that would trigger the little bell that sounded off with each customer's arrival.

She released the door, raced to the counter. She launched herself over it, landing quietly on the large black rubber antifatigue mat as the bell jingled. Crawling quickly, she made herself as small as possible at the end of the counter closest to the front of the store, where she would be able to watch for the deputy's arrival.

Assuming she was still breathing when that happened.

The near silent tread of rubber soles on the shiny tile floor blasted across her senses.

The guy with the gun was coming.

She didn't have to see him to know he would be scanning the aisles and surveying the parking area around his truck. He'd heard the bell on the door.

He stopped at the front of the counter and leaned across, expecting to find the trouble hidden behind it.

Meg didn't dare breathe.

She had, at best, one shot at this.

As he walked toward the end of the counter where she was hiding, her muscles bunched in anticipation of lunging for him.

Tension vibrated inside her, fingers tightening on her knife.

A scream from the back of the building stopped his momentum.

"Help me!" Jennifer's trembling voice. "Please help me."

He swore, and that single, muttered word told Meg that he was nearly on top of her—just around the corner of the counter—maybe two feet away from her position.

Meg dared to move her head, leaning back just far enough to see him from the shoulders up. His back was turned to her. He was torn between shutting up his hostage and ensuring no one else was inside the store with him.

Jennifer screamed again.

Meg readied to move.

Now or never.

She shot upward.

He twisted…the weapon in his hand leveled on Meg.

The logo of a rock band on his tee, ragged jeans and biker boots flashed through her brain in that single second before she propelled herself forward. She swiped her knife across his throat. Twisted her body into a roll. Hit the tile and rolled.

The gun went off.

The ping of the bullet hitting the floor next to her had her scrambling farther away.

Then the gun bounced on the floor.

Meg scrambled to her feet.

His hands were at his throat, blood spewed between his fingers and flowed down his torso in a river of red.

His gaze connected with Meg's for a split second—damn, he was young—before he crumpled to the floor.

No matter that he was a goner, she kicked the gun across the floor before rushing toward the storage room. She bypassed the restrooms and the entrance to the cooler and rushed through the open door that led into the back, into the storeroom.

Jennifer, her clothes half ripped off her body, huddled in the floor next to boxes of paper products.

Her left wrist was tied to a metal pipe that snaked up the wall. Meg cut her loose and then tucked her knife away. She reached toward the terrified young woman. "You're okay now, Jennifer. Deputy Battles is on the way."

Jennifer's eyes remained wide with fear. Tears and mucus streamed down her face. "He…he…"

"He won't hurt you now."

Meg sat down on the floor next to her and held her until help arrived.

Chapter Two

The blue lights from the two sheriff's department SUVs throbbed in the night, sending flashes through the glass-fronted store. Meg couldn't say for sure how long it had taken for Deputy Battles to arrive. Long enough for the adrenaline that had been coursing through her body to recede, leaving her to face the reality of what had just gone down in a colder, harsher light. Long enough for her to understand that there was a strong possibility this would change everything.

There had been no alternative. She'd only done what she had to do.

Another deputy had cordoned off the half of the parking lot nearest the entrance with yellow crime scene tape. A sedan bearing the county's CSI team logo had arrived maybe half an hour ago. The sergeant, probably the leader of the team, had glanced at Meg as he entered the shop.

The coroner had taken the body away a few minutes after that. There was a lot of blood on the floor.

A *lot* of blood.

Meg blinked and turned her face away to prevent staring at the spot on the shiny tile floor where the perp had expired. She hadn't seen that much blood in a while.

She'd hoped never to see or to be involved with this sort of thing ever again.

This was so, so not good.

Her nerves jangled as she allowed the idea of what had just happened to sink in a little deeper.

Not good at all.

Damn it.

The perp had been identified as Zyair Jones, a career criminal from just across the state line. Though only twenty-five, he had a long line of offenses, not the least of which was armed robbery and sexual assault. Jennifer might not feel like it just now, but she was lucky to be alive. Men like the perp who'd dragged her into that storeroom typically escalated, and judging by his extensive rap sheet, an escalation had been due any time now.

Meg shifted in the stiff plastic chair next to the counter at the farthest end of the shop where she'd been sequestered by Deputy Battles. Since there were no other seats in the building except for the one she'd seen at the desk in the storeroom, she supposed this one was for the clerk on duty to take a load off when the opportunity presented itself. When someone like Jennifer was on duty alone, going to a breakroom was not really an option. The entrance would need to be locked for her to even go to the restroom for a personal relief break. Meg imagined the boss didn't want that door locked any more than necessary.

The owner had been called and, like the rest of those interested in what had occurred tonight, waited beyond the crime scene perimeter. She'd spotted the lady who owned the diner and the man who'd opened the book shop. There were several others, but none she recognized from this distance.

Meg had already given Battles a quick overview of what happened while the paramedics examined Jennifer. But he would be back when he completed his questioning of the victim. Meg had watched his face as she answered the questions he posed. He'd tried not to look surprised when she'd told him about swiping the knife across the guy's throat, but he'd failed to keep his face clear of the reaction. There were other questions he would have for the next round. Like why did she carry a knife? What had prompted her to react so violently? What had made her think to slash the truck tires before coming inside? Etcetera.

She gave her head a little shake. Providing answers that would assuage any concerns or uncertainties he had would be easy enough for now, but the notion of what she'd done would linger in his thoughts. Every time he saw her from this moment forward, he would remember this night. The neighboring shop owners would talk among themselves about how she'd been able to take down the would-be robber and rapist. And there was no question what Jones had intended. The cash from the register had been in his pocket, and he'd torn at Jennifer's clothes while he regaled her with his intentions. Still, there would be talk.

Nothing she could do about that.

For now, she was just thankful she was seated far enough away from that expansive wall of glass to avoid the prying eyes. The last thing she needed was someone taking her photo and putting it on the net or, God forbid, in the news.

"Meg."

She glanced up at the sound of her name. Battles stood at the entrance to the short corridor that led into the back. He motioned for her to come with him.

Careful to keep her back to the front of the shop, she did as he asked.

Now for the second round of questioning.

When she reached him, he turned and walked with her toward the storeroom door. "One of the deputies from the Dread Hollow substation is driving Jennifer home, but she wanted to see you before leaving."

"Is she okay?" Evidently so, but asking was the appropriate response.

"She's shaken up," he said, "as you can imagine, but she sustained nothing more than minor physical injuries."

She got it. The horror of what happened would be the only mark that lingered. For how long would be entirely up to Jennifer and her ability to bounce back from trauma without developing PTSD. Hopefully she would be one of the lucky ones. With the right kind of support, it was possible.

When Meg walked through the door, Jennifer rushed to her and hugged her hard. "Thank you so much for saving me." She drew back. Tears flooded down her cheeks. "Deputy Battles told me I was so lucky that you spotted the trouble and came to help since he couldn't get here fast enough." She looked away a moment. "He said he was going to kill me."

"But he didn't get the chance," Meg assured her, then she produced a smile. "And what kind of neighbor would I be if I didn't help?"

Jennifer's lips quivered as she managed a dim smile. "Thank you." She scrubbed at her face with her hands before resting her gaze on Meg's once more. "You saved my life."

Meg nodded. "We both got lucky."

"Your parents are waiting for you," Battles said. "You go on home and take it easy for a while, like I said. And call that counselor."

Jennifer promised she would then the other deputy ushered her away. When the back door closed behind the two, Battles said, "Let's go over a couple more things, and then I'll have Deputy Porch escort you back to your place."

Porch was the deputy from Dread Hollow who'd just left with Jennifer. Meg made it a point to know all members of law enforcement in the area. Knowledge was power as well as protection.

"That won't be necessary," Meg insisted. "I'll be less conspicuous if I take the long way around through the alley and avoid all those folks gathered out front."

"You're not worried about going that long way around in the dark?"

Her answer had surprised him, and now that nagging little suspicion that something was off here was bugging him again. There were people who noticed little things like that, particularly cops and those working in the fields where the extra effort of paying attention were crucial. A good cop didn't miss much.

"No, sir," she insisted, mentally scrambling for the right answer to head off a deepening of his curiosity. "I take my runs at night along those same paths. I've never bumped into any trouble."

This was pretty much true. Though she had been observed by a bear once. A fox more than once. And a coyote twice. Never another human, which is what she suspected he meant. She had no fear of the local wildlife, just a healthy respect. That was all any animal needed. She spent so much time with dogs she imagined she smelled more like a dog than a human on those rare encounters with wildlife anyway.

Battles nodded slowly as if he wasn't entirely sure he was okay with the idea but couldn't think of a good enough excuse to argue her point. Finally, he hitched his head toward the desk and chair. "Why don't you have a seat at the desk, and we'll go over a few things, and then you're free to go."

Meg returned his nod. "Sure."

This was where things would get tricky.

She walked to the desk, pulled out the chair and settled into it. Same hard plastic as the other one. Most likely, the owner didn't want any employee getting too comfortable sitting down. Battles leaned against the wall next to the desk. He looked exhausted as he flipped back a few pages in his notepad. He'd probably been on duty well past his shift at this point.

"You stated," he began, "that you were at your window and noticed the trouble across the way." He lifted his gaze to hers. "Meaning here."

"That's right." She made a sound, a kind of soft laugh. "I'm a watcher. Birds, animals and people. I keep a pair of binoculars at the window. My apartment upstairs faces the street. In the mornings when I first get up and at night before I go to bed. It's relaxing. I like watching the world around me—no matter where I am. It's a habit I developed during all my travels. You'd be surprised what you notice just watching the world go by."

He grunted an acknowledgment as he made a note of her answer.

As far as anyone in this town knew, she had spent most of her adult life traveling the world. This was the first place she had stayed for more than six months, she had told anyone who asked. But at almost thirty-five, she had decided it was time to settle down. She'd always loved animals, and going into the business of taking care of them was the perfect career. The cover story had sounded good to her and, so far, to whomever she'd told it.

"Is that why you carry a survivalist type knife?"

This was the biggest sticking point for the deputy. Understandable. A woman carrying a knife like the one she had wasn't the norm.

"It is. I've never been very fond of guns, but I've spent a lot of nights in a sleeping bag on the ground under the stars. Keeping a knife handy felt like a healthy habit. These days, it helps with all sorts of menial tasks, like opening all those boxes delivered to my shop. Once in a while, a pet will get hung up in its restraint loop, and I never want to cause an animal anxiety by taking the time to untangle it. I'd much rather just cut the restraint and start fresh."

Battles made another note before meeting her eyes once more. "So, you don't carry it for protection?"

Meg turned her hands up. "I suppose I do. I mean, I have it with me on my runs, and if confronted by trouble, I would do what I had to. Like tonight. But injuring anything or anyone—much less taking a life— is never something I want to do. I'd much prefer to avoid the trouble altogether."

The deputy's brow furrowed as he considered her for a few seconds more. "Just one last question."

Meg braced herself. This would be the one that required the most finagling.

"Why didn't you stab him? Why go for the throat that way?" He shrugged. "Just seems like an unexpected move for someone such as yourself."

Meaning a woman who wasn't a cop or self-defense expert. If Jones hadn't been wielding a gun, she would certainly have gone a different, perhaps even less lethal route. But her only hope had been to go for the swiftest deadly strike.

Meg took a moment, although she already had her answer prepared. "I was attacked once." She drew in a deep breath. "A very long time ago. After that, I decided it would be in my best interest if I took a self-defense course. According to the instructor, when your weapon of choice is a knife and you are faced with certain death, it's best to go for the jugular. Anything else is like trying to swat a fly with a tennis racket. Too much leeway for a potential miss."

He held her gaze for a long moment without responding. Obviously he wanted more.

"He had a gun pointed at my head. If I'd tried to stab him, I would have been dead before the point of my knife pierced his skin. My only viable option was to lunge, swipe and go into a rolling dive for the floor in hopes of avoiding the shot he would no doubt pull off."

Battles gave one of those vague nods. "But how did you slit his throat before he could fire the weapon?"

A reasonable question from a man who thought Meg to be a throwback to the days of hippies and flower children. She supposed she did sort of dress the part. Old jeans, vintage tees. She kept her long dark hair in a braid. It was a good cover.

"I was hunkered behind the counter," she explained, "as I said earlier. When he reached the end of the corner, his weapon aimed at me, Jennifer suddenly screamed for help. He turned to stare toward the storeroom—instinct, I suppose—and I took the only opportunity I believed I would have."

A firmer nod this time. "You were lucky."

"I was lucky." She blinked. "I'm just sorry I had to...do what I did."

Battles tucked his notepad away. "I'm sorry to have to confiscate your knife and scabbard, but I'm sure you've watched enough TV and movies to know we have to keep all evidence until the investigation is concluded."

"I understand." She had a backup. No need to tell him that part. For now, she was just thankful not to have aroused his suspicions further.

"I'll be in touch if we have more questions." He straightened from the wall. "You sure you don't want someone to walk you home?"

Meg stood, relief sliding through her body, immediately followed by exhaustion. It was late and she was tired. "No thanks. You've got your hands full here. No need to take someone away from their work to walk me around the block."

"You did a good thing, Meg," he said softly. "I know this may be difficult to live with for a while, and you'll question yourself over what you had to do, but, bottom line, you did the right thing and there's no question in my mind that you saved Jennifer's life. You're a hero."

Oh, good grief. She was not a hero and the last thing she wanted was that label in the report. "I just did what anyone in my shoes would have done." She shrugged. "It's not like the guy gave me a lot of choices."

"Still," Battles insisted, "you took a great risk, and now it's time to take care of you. See a counselor. This was a traumatizing night, and the full impact won't have set in yet. Taking a life—no matter the circumstances—comes with a truckload of emotional baggage. Don't ignore the impact to your psyche."

"Thanks, I'll keep that in mind."

Deputy Porch called for Battles, and before he could say more to Meg, she turned and walked toward the back door. The door closed behind her, and she took a moment to draw in a chestful of air. She closed her eyes and drew in another breath, exhaled it, then she started to walk. She weaved her way through the woods for the short distance before it turned into the narrow alleyway that lined the back of the old shops. Rather than step into the alley, she kept to the woods. The going was rougher, but the likelihood of running into anyone was greatly diminished.

When she reached the end of the first block of the old shops, she made her way up to the alley and around the corner to the side street. At the end of each of the four blocks that constituted the old town portion of Piney Woods, a short, narrow cross street led into residential areas. There weren't that many houses actually used as homes. Two had been transformed into bed-and-breakfast operations, one was a doctor's office, another was a dental clinic and most of the others were now retail shops.

The few that remained residential holdouts were those of founding families. The annual Christmas tours featured those homes, and members of the families told stories of how their ancestors had come to choose this portion of the mountain as home. All the shops participated. Last Christmas, even Meg had opened her shop to the tour. She'd had her employees do the hosting. Putting herself in the limelight was not something she liked doing.

Not to mention it was dangerous.

Not going there.

A glance down the boulevard and Meg surveyed the crowd that still lingered in the Gas and Go parking lot. Emergency lights still strobed in the darkness. Excitement like this almost never happened in Piney Woods. Folks would be out until it was wrapped up in hopes of learning the full details.

The idea that trouble had shown up tonight worried Meg just a little.

Not that she really thought the dead guy who'd attempted to rob the Gas and Go had anything to do with her past. *Nah.* The idea was pretty ridiculous, in fact. Frankly, he'd been an amateur. His long list of crimes indicated nothing more than a scumbag who preferred not to work for a living. He opted to take what he wanted because he was too damned lazy to earn it.

She'd met plenty of stone-cold killers in her life, and he had not been one of them.

Sadly, however, had her reflexes been any rustier, she would be the one dead on that slab in the Hamilton County Morgue. She'd barely outmaneuvered the thuggish punk.

"You gotta stay in shape, Lewis," she muttered as she ducked into the alley on her side of the block. It had been just over fifteen months since she'd been in a position to need to protect herself. She imagined even if it had been fifteen years, muscle memory would have had her doing the same thing. There were some things that couldn't be forgotten. But speed and accuracy were another story. Those required regular training.

Beyond ready to get home, she walked faster now. She wanted to wash the night's events off her skin and burn her damned clothes.

When she at last reached her shop, she entered the code into the gate and stepped into the fenced perimeter of her back yard. The area was a like a kid's playground, except the equipment was designed for dogs. There were a couple of doggie ramps and slides. Tunnels and balance beams. Shade houses. Her favorites were the water fountains and the toy boxes. And she hadn't overlooked the cats she served when designing the playground. Two state-of-the-art cat condos had been installed. A little something for everyone.

At the back door, she entered the code, and the lock released. Once inside, she toed off her sneakers and stripped off her clothes. She frowned, remembered she'd shut off the ringer on her cell. She switched it back on and tucked the device into the waistband of her panties and walked to the laundry area, where she grabbed a couple of garbage bags. For now, hiding the clothes would have to do. She was too tired to burn them tonight. Besides, the last thing she needed was the crowd at the Gas and Go seeing smoke behind her shop. She'd take care of it tomorrow, but she didn't want the animals picking up the scent of the dead guy. She double-bagged the trash and stuffed it into the front-loading washing machine and closed the door.

She made it up the stairs before her cell erupted into the short, soft bursts of her chosen ringtone. Too tired to answer anything but a true emergency, she tugged the phone free of her waistband and checked the screen.

Griff.

He'd already called seven times. She should have noticed when she turned the ringer back on. Apparently, she'd been too tired, and no doubt he'd heard about the trouble.

She hit Accept and said, "Hey. What're you doing up so late?"

"Checking on you after learning about the robbery at the Gas and Go."

Pain arced through her shoulder as she reached for the nightshirt draped on her bed. She grimaced. "I'm okay. Just about to go to bed."

She didn't like blowing him off. Avery "Griff" Griffin was a good friend—one of the first she'd made when she moved here last year. She liked him. Maybe too much. But the less he knew about this, the better.

Like that was going to happen. Griff and Deputy Ernie Battles had been best friends since they were kids.

"Well, that's a shame because I'm at your front door."

She closed her eyes and held back a sigh. "Why didn't you say so? I'll be right down."

Meg considered changing out of her nightshirt, but she needed it to back up her story. Besides, it wasn't like Griff hadn't seen her in shorts and tank tops. Not that different really. That thought introduced a long line of images into her head that she could have done without just now. Memories of Griff pulling off his shirt during a long hot afternoon of work at his farm. A T-shirt plastered to his chest after helping to give a dozen dogs baths.

Not somewhere she needed to linger. She exiled the memories. They both loved animals and worked hard to rescue as many as possible, but that common bond was as far as the thing between them needed to go.

She hustled down the stairs and padded silently across the cool tile floor. He waited at the front entrance, looking all sleep tousled and far too sexy.

Don't think about it.

Without turning on a light so as not to draw attention, she unlocked the door and opened it. "Wild night," she said with a glance at the ongoing spectacle at the Gas and Go.

"Yeah." He closed and locked the door.

So, he planned to stay a while. Which meant he'd already heard most of the story about her part in what happened. The downside to living in a small town—everyone knew everyone else. Nothing stayed secret for more than a minute.

"You want a beer?" She folded her arms over her chest.

He shook his head. "You gonna tell me what happened?"

"First." She held up a finger. "There's something I need to show you."

She turned and headed for the kennels. He followed. No need for her to look back and check, she could feel his closeness. This would buy her some time to calm her jangling nerves. A few minutes of distraction to take the edge off.

As she entered the doggie hotel—as she liked to call the kennels—Raymond raised his head. He still lay next to the abandoned beagle's kennel.

Meg crouched down and gave Raymond a scratch between the ears. "Hey, boy."

Griff eased down next to her and reached over to do the same. He and Raymond had a very close relationship. This did not help Meg's ability to keep the man at a safe distance. The scent of his aftershave—

even at this hour—made her want to lean closer and take a long, deep breath.

He smiled at Raymond, then shifted his attention to the beagle. "Hey there."

"She's about eight or nine," Meg said. "Her name is Pepper. She has some health issues. Lonnie's going to run tests. Try to get to the bottom of the situation."

"Where'd you find her?"

His gaze locked on hers, and for a moment, Meg couldn't speak. She chalked it up to the insane night she'd had. Truth was, he did that to her sometimes. His hair was that blond color that wasn't really all that fair but was still way too light to call brown. More of a mix of caramel and gold. His eyes were the kind of gold you rarely saw. So pale, so distinct. But the trouble didn't lay in those gorgeous eyes or in the six feet of perfectly formed masculinity. No. The trouble was his incredible kind and giving nature, especially toward animals. Meg had never met anyone quite like him.

The fact that she was seriously attracted to him was not such a big surprise, all things considered, but she respected him and just plain old liked him in ways she had never expected to like anyone. The latter was terrifying on some level. She'd never been attracted to anyone in the way she was to this man. It was as much intellectual as it was physical.

Griff was making her soft, making her want things she could never have.

Somehow she had to remedy that situation. Problem was, she hadn't figured out a way to do that—not in the twelve months she had been here.

Don't think about it right now.

She pulled her mind back to the moment and the question he'd asked. "The owner couldn't take care of her anymore and left her at my door with a note."

Griff smiled. "Then it's someone who knows you and realizes what a good person you are."

She looked away from that incredible smile and focused on Pepper. "Except I don't have the space for allowing the reputation for taking on extra pets to become a common belief. I wish I did." This was the truth, at least most of it. She would take them all if she could. The problem was if she had to disappear—and that was always a possibility—what would become of them?

She couldn't live with the probable answer to that question.

"I've got the space. When she's on her feet—" he turned to Meg, the pull of his eyes forcing her to look at him "—I'll take her."

She managed a smile, mostly because the effort prevented her from analyzing the details of his face more deeply. The lips...the jawline. *Stop.* "You already have a lot of animals, Griff."

He chuckled. "Doesn't matter. I have a big farm with a barn big enough for my herd of dogs and cows and horses—as well as plenty more."

"Not to mention no shortage of cats and chickens."

His smile turned to a grin. "Those too."

He hadn't purchased or been gifted a single animal that lived on his farm. All had been abandoned. Every cow, every horse. Even the chickens. Folks would call him when someone had moved away and just left one or more animals. Griff would go pick them up and bring them home. If they were sick or injured, he would nurse them back to health, and there they would stay. It was the perfect life for the animals and for him. Meg could never tell anyone, but it was her dream life.

Not ever going to happen, she reminded herself.

"Why don't you tell me about what happened over there?"

This was the question she'd dreaded. She pushed to her feet. "I need a beer."

He stood. "That bad, huh?"

He already knew the answer. Ernie might not be able to give him ever little detail because of the ongoing investigation, but he would have passed along all he could.

"Yeah. That bad."

The worst part about Griff knowing was the idea that it would likely change his opinion of her—and not for the good.

Griff was the first person in her adult life—besides her parents—whose opinion mattered so very much to her.

This was bad, and nothing in her vast survival repertoire gave her any suggestion on how to stop the momentum.

Chapter Three

Griffin Residence
Sundown Road
Sunday, May 5, 8:30 a.m.

"Listen up," Griff said to the dogs eagerly waiting at the doors of their kennels. "Dr. Howell is coming this morning for checkups, shots or whatever any of you need. I expect you all to behave."

Sad, gloomy eyes peered up at him as if they'd understood every word.

"Don't give me that," he argued. "You behave yourselves and you all get treats."

Ears perked up and tails wagged just a little, and he smiled.

"All right then. You'll be staying in your kennels until after Dr. Howell has seen you, so just chill for a while."

As he walked away, the animals began to settle in for the wait. Though some had been abused and all were castoffs, they trained easily and well. Even Petey, the newest arrival. Griff gave the old bloodhound a nod as he passed his kennel. Petey had settled down, following the lead of the others.

Griff couldn't remember a time when he wasn't surrounded by dogs and other animals. Every morning he spent hours feeding and filling water bowls and troughs. But he loved every minute of it. He shook his head at the idea that he'd ever thought for one minute he could be happy in the world of high finance in the big city. But as his grandmother had often told him, if he hadn't given it a go, he would still be wondering. Now he knew.

Outside the veterinarian's truck had arrived. "Morning," Lonnie announced as he headed Griff's way.

Griff opened the gate to the large pen that surrounded the barn. "Morning, Doc. The day been good to you so far?"

Lonnie chuckled. "As good as it can when you've got a calf in distress during delivery. We had a rough go of it for a bit, but luckily, we managed all right. Mama and baby are just fine. Henry's wife even made me breakfast."

Henry Bauer was a neighboring farmer. His family had owned their farm almost as long as Griff's had.

"Good to hear." Griff gestured to the doghouse, which was actually a two-thousand-square-foot building with forty dog kennels and a storeroom. The kennels were all inside, but there were plenty of windows, and each kennel had access to this large fenced area in back of the building. "Your patients are ready. If you need me, let me know."

"I always look forward to your crew. And I appreciate you letting me come on a Sunday morning. The better part of the upcoming week is looking a little crowded."

Griff understood. Lonnie's partner had retired due to health issues, and so far he hadn't found a replacement. The man was swamped. "No problem. I'm just thrilled you could get to us."

Lonnie paused before moving on. "By the way, I may know someone who's interested in the bloodhound."

Griff liked nothing better than finding loving families for the animals, but *loving* was the key word. "You made them aware that she's old?"

"I did. He already has a dozen of his own. Like you, he likes giving them a good life—age or condition is irrelevant. Trust me, Griff, he'll take good care of her when you're ready to let her go. And she'll be with others like herself."

How could he say no? Bloodhounds were pack dogs. She would be happiest with a group of her own kind. "Sounds good. Have him give me a call at his convenience."

"Will do."

Lonnie wandered on to the kennels. Griff was caught up for now, so he headed to the house. Meg had promised to come and have a late breakfast with him. She'd managed to persuade him to go home last night without providing details about what happened at the Gas and Go. He hadn't been thrilled about the idea, but she'd been exhausted, so he'd given in. Part of him had wanted to park outside her place and keep watch all night. But that wouldn't have helped. She wasn't in any danger. If he'd ever had any doubts about her taking care of herself, he had none now. He was the one who had an issue.

He wanted to take their friendship to a different level, but she insisted she wasn't ready for that sort of relationship just now. Not exactly the answer he wanted to hear, but he couldn't deny understanding where she was at. He'd been there. Leaving Nashville eight years ago hadn't been just about being unhappy with his career choice. His whole life had been turned upside down when the woman he'd expected to marry and spend the rest of his life with had announced she had a new vision for the rest of her own. Even more surprising was the reality of how little he'd missed her. Then had come the unexpected relief. Looking back, he realized he had come way too close to making the mistake of his life.

He walked through the back door and into the old farmhouse kitchen that badly needed an update. He hung his hat on the hook by the door and headed to the coffee maker. He'd had a quick cup at 5:30 a.m. this morning, but he needed another desperately just now. While he waited through the hissing of the machine doing its thing, he considered the cabinets, counters and appliances that were the same as when he'd been a kid. Until recently, he hadn't thought much of the aged interior. It was all serviceable. Clean. What else did a man need? Except his sister had suggested he might want to update if he ever expected to lure in potential wife material. What woman, she'd insisted, wanted to see herself in this kitchen?

Griff shook his head and barely restrained a laugh. His sister, on the other hand, couldn't stop renovating. Louise Griffin Alvarez had married a mere twelve years ago, and already she'd renovated her house twice. Good thing her husband had a sense of humor and a healthy bank account.

Griff loved his little sister. She was so much like their mother. In fact, Louise had built an in-law suite during her last renovation, and their mom loved living with her daughter and her grandkids. Louise teased that if Griff would just get around to having kids of his own, maybe he too could enjoy some nana time. Griff glanced around the old kitchen and couldn't stop the flood of images and sounds that echoed in his brain. He and his sister had been happy growing up here. The only bad memory was when he'd found his father down by the pond, and even that one wasn't all bad. His father had died the way he'd wanted to. He'd been working in the yard and gotten overheated. He'd taken a break in the shade by the pond—one of his favorite places.

Taking walks down memory lane happened more and more often these days. Maybe because his sister reminded him every chance she got that he wasn't getting any younger. And it was hard not to visit the past when he lived in the house where he'd grown up. His grandfather had built the home and the barn. His father had grown up here too. His parents had planned to live here until they passed, just as his grandparents had. Though things hadn't worked out exactly as planned, Griff intended to go for that same goal. He just hadn't expected to do it alone. When he'd come back eight years ago, he'd figured that eventually he'd meet someone and start the rest of his life. So far that had not happened—he hadn't even come close. He shook his head and pushed away from the counter.

He scrubbed a hand over his face. Maybe he did need to renovate. Shake things up. New paint colors and all that.

Too bad the woman his heart seemed intent on wasn't interested and likely wouldn't be impressed by a shiny new kitchen.

Speaking of Meg, he spotted her truck coming up the drive. Meg had insisted on bringing the food. All he had to do was provide hot coffee and orange juice. The scent of the fresh brew lingered in the room. He opened the fridge door, grabbed the carton of orange juice and placed it on the counter, where he arranged a couple of glasses and mugs. He considered pouring a cup of coffee to take to Lonnie, but the knock on his front door derailed the notion.

He ran his fingers through his hair, took a breath and headed through the home. The place was a typical farmhouse. Two stories. All the bedrooms and a bath upstairs. The common rooms and a half bath that was added in the fifties downstairs. Nothing fancy. Hardwoods on the floors. Painted plaster on the walls. All in need of a refresh, according to his sister.

Still, the place suited him. He was happiest in a pair of jeans and boots. He wore a cowboy hat the way his father and grandfather had. When his ex-fiancée insisted the hat had to be saved for the proper occasion, he should have realized things between them would never work. He'd grown up with cows and horses and chickens and such. The proper boots and hat were more important than any other attire he'd worn.

Meg liked his hat. He smiled at the memory of her saying so.

He opened the door and the woman standing on his porch made him smile even wider. Meg Lewis had the brownest eyes he'd ever seen. So dark they were like gazing into midnight. And the hair. He loved her hair. Long, dark and thick, but she almost never allowed it to hang free. It was always in a single braid hanging down her back all the way to her waist or draped over one shoulder with a cute little ribbon tied at the end.

Today there was no ribbon.

His gaze roamed back up the pink tee that sported images of blooming botanicals then to her face. She smiled, and that alone had his heart stuttering.

He almost laughed at the reality of just how pathetic he was. Maybe it was the idea that forty was looming in the not-so-distant future and the wife and kids he'd expected to have were still nothing more than an expectation. Or maybe it was the idea that he'd finally met the *one*, and she only wanted to be friends.

Meg held up a brown bag with the diner's logo on the front. "Katie insisted we try her new breakfast burritos."

Griff hummed a note of anticipation. "If Katie made them, they'll be good." He hitched his head. "Come on in."

Meg stepped inside. "How's your herd this morning?"

"Nervous."

"Guess so. I saw Lonnie's truck out there."

"Yep." His stomach rumbled. "Man, those burritos smell good."

MEG COULDN'T AGREE MORE. She hoped the food would help stave off his questions about last night. She'd tossed and turned the few hours she'd spent in bed wondering how to get past the questions he would no doubt have. To some degree, Griff saw through her facade. His ability to view her so clearly made her a little nervous.

Deputy Battles had been happy to accept her explanation of what happened—or at least he appeared to do so. But Griff would have other concerns. Like how had she managed to react so exactly? How had she recognized how deep the knife should go to inflict the necessary result?

Worse, she hadn't been able to suppress the worries about her photo ending up in the media. All this time, she had been so careful to ensure she stayed below the radar. To her knowledge, not a single photo had been taken of her since her arrival in Piney Woods. But if this rescue of hers picked up too much steam in a slow news cycle, the reporters involved would go to great lengths to find something on her.

If that happened...

Just stop. She cleared her head. She had no control over what others did. All Meg could do was take this one step at a time. Maybe the whole thing would fizzle out today. Maybe Griff wouldn't ask as many questions as she feared he would. And maybe he would accept her answers without wanting additional clarifications.

Yeah, right. She'd never get that lucky.

Whatever happened, she would do what she had to. The trouble was Avery Griffin had spent seven years as a forensic auditor in one of Nashville's top financial groups. He was trained to look beyond what he saw and to find the reasons behind the results. Actually, she suspected his university training had little to do with this ability. She firmly believed the man instinctively saw what others didn't. For the past year she had worked extra hard to keep him at arm's length.

Not an easy task. She took in his crisp white cotton shirt and faded blue jeans. The boots…she resisted the urge to sigh. Too distracting, too desirable. The man just got under her skin somehow.

He was just too good-looking. Too nice. Too… *good*.

In the kitchen, he gestured to the counter. "Coffee's ready. Orange juice is handy."

Meg placed the bag of burritos on the table. She liked this house. The big farm-style kitchen with the table in the center made her want to bake bread, and she'd never baked bread in her life. It just felt so homey. "Should we invite Lonnie? I'm sure we have enough food."

Griff frowned before he seemed to catch himself and fix his smile back into place. "He mentioned that Mrs. Bauer made him breakfast this morning. He was helping out with the birth of a calf."

"You have a sick animal, or is he here for routine examinations?" She opened the bag and removed the warm wrapped goodies. It was Sunday after all. Not the usual office hours even for a country vet.

"Just vaccinations and checkups." He poured two steaming mugs of coffee. "He has a big week coming up and wanted to get a head start."

He didn't have to ask how Meg took her coffee. They'd had coffee together enough times that he knew she liked it black. They'd made fast friends only a few weeks after she got her shop going. He'd gone out of his way to send business in her direction. He brought two or three of his dogs each week. She doubted he'd ever bothered with a groomer before, but he was thoughtful like that.

By the time she had the food on the plates he'd provided, she was salivating at the delicious smells of peppers and onions and cheeses. The eggs and spicy sausage and all those other juicy ingredients were rolled into homemade tortillas. She was ravenous this morning. She wouldn't mention this though since most people wouldn't likely understand her having any sort of appetite after what happened last night.

Griff placed the mugs of coffee on the table and filled two glasses with orange juice, then they sat.

"You feeling okay this morning?" he asked as he unwrapped his burrito.

His first question was simple enough. She relaxed a little. "I'm good. Not as sore as I expected after that dive to the floor." Realizing her missed opportunity, she added, "I'm working on not thinking about the other part."

"I'm sure that part will just take time."

"Hope so."

They ate for a time. Whatever question he had next waited. Suited Meg. The burrito was so good she devoured it in record time. Felt a little guilty about wolfing it down. She toyed with her napkin a bit, finished off her orange juice and considered whether she wanted another cup of coffee. The man brewed good coffee. Or maybe she'd go for another burrito.

"You ready to talk about it?"

No. Absolutely not. But she had promised to talk to him this morning, so refusing was not an option. Not to mention how worried he looked. Her goal was to alleviate his concerns without prompting his curiosity. Always a fine line.

"Sure." She took a deep breath and launched into her practiced story. "You know how I love watching my little part of town. I could just sit at my front window and watch all day—or night—long."

"You spotted the trouble," he suggested as he reached for a second burrito.

"I usually take a look before I go to bed." She made a face, a bit embarrassed. "It's just a silly routine of mine. I swear I'm not nosy or some sort of peeping perv."

"I always take a walk around outside before going to bed. Check on the animals." He laughed. "Say good night. So I understand."

He really was such a nice guy. She would never want him to know how she'd had to lie her way into this life. "I do that too—say good night, I mean. Some folks might think that's a little strange, but it feels like the right thing to do."

His smile faded, and he held her gaze for a long moment. Her pulse reacted. "I think that's part of why I like you so much, Megan Lewis. You're my kind of people."

The want in his eyes, the sound of desire in his voice—every ounce of strength she possessed was required not to give in. How many times had she thought about taking him to her bed? Or joining him in his? God, she didn't even remember how long it had been since she'd had sex. Forever…it seemed.

But she would not—could not drag this man more deeply into her life. The potential for a bad outcome was far too great a risk.

Friends. They could be friends.

"Anyway," she went on, "I spotted the guy with the gun and immediately called Deputy Battles. He was ten minutes out and there was no one else, so I did what I had to do." She stared into her empty coffee mug for a long moment. "By the time I got across the street, the guy was dragging Jennifer into the storeroom. I knew what would happen. I had to do something. She didn't have ten minutes."

The unfinished second burrito went back onto his plate. He reached for a napkin and wiped his hands as if needing time before speaking. "Ernie said you saved her life."

Meg shrugged. "I'm just glad I spotted what was happening."

"I take it," he ventured, "you've had self-defense or survival instruction of some sort." He glanced away. "Ernie mentioned you'd been attacked before."

She'd known the two would have this discussion. Not only had they been best friends since their school days, they'd been on the basketball team together. Theirs was a tight bond.

"Mugged," she said, going for the less complicated scenario. "He roughed me up a little. Bruises, broken wrist. I decided that was never going to happen again, so… I made myself smarter, more prepared for the unexpected."

The relief on his face was palpable. "I think that's smart. I've urged my sister to do the same. Everyone should know how to protect him- or herself."

"It's important." Meg had met Louise. And his mother. He'd taken her to Thanksgiving dinner last year. He'd wanted to take her to the family's Christmas gathering as well, but she'd pretended to be sick. Family Christmases were far too intimate.

Her decision hadn't been about not wanting to spend time with his family. Like him, they were all very nice. It was about protecting herself and him from the mistake he so badly wanted to make.

She could not be what he wanted, and to pretend otherwise would only do harm.

"I need you to promise me something, Meg."

She held her breath. Hoped this was not going to be one of those things that would make remaining friends even more difficult.

"I'll try," she offered.

"Next time, call me. Let me help."

That she could agree to. "I will. There just wasn't time last night. It all happened so quickly."

"I understand, but I want to try and be there whenever you need me for whatever reason."

She relaxed just a little. Maybe he wasn't going to go after answers the way she had feared. "I appreciate that."

He cleaned up the remains of their breakfast while she washed their mugs and glasses. She adored the vintage sink with its attached drainboard. It was all so homey. So comfortable.

"You can never change this sink," she said as she dried her hands. "It's amazing."

He leaned against the counter and grinned. "Don't ever say that in front of my sister. She thinks I need to gut the place and have all new everything installed."

Meg's mouth dropped open in dismay. "No. This kitchen is perfect. The cabinets are perfectly imperfect. I love the pale green color." She put a hand to her chest. "And the stove. It's a Wedgewood. You can never ever change the stove either."

"I'm glad you like it."

The amusement in his tone and in those gold eyes made her feel far too warm. "Sorry," she offered, "I get a little carried away when people talk about ruining something as awesome as this kitchen."

"Since we're on the subject," he said, "what about the paint?"

It was yellow. Nice. Very light. "This must have been your mother's favorite color."

He grinned. "It was. She repainted it this same color every few years."

Meg's cell sounded off from the back pocket of her jeans. Saved her from having to say that she'd never really cared for yellow. "Excuse me a moment." She checked the screen. Jodie Edwards. "It's Jodie. I have to take this."

Griff knew both her employees, Jodie Edwards and Dottie Cowart. One or the other usually worked with Meg on Sunday afternoons to get the weekly deep cleaning done, but today they'd suggested the two of them handle the shop for Meg. After last night's misadventures, Meg hadn't argued. They would also hang around for the pickup of the boarded animals. Prevented Meg from having to answer the questions the owners would no doubt have. Frankly, she was glad to have the day off.

She accepted the call. "Hey, Jodie. What's up?"

"There's a couple of reporters hanging around outside," Jodie whispered. "One from the *Chattanooga Times* and one from the *Tennessean*. They've knocked on the door wanting to talk to you."

Meg suppressed a groan. She had been afraid of this. "Tell them not only are we closed but that I won't be around today." She made a face. Tried to think how she would manage to stay out of sight until this whole thing blew over.

"Actually, I was thinking that I can handle things for a couple of days," Jodie offered. "Dottie is happy to come in and help if I need her."

Meg wilted with relief. "That would be great, Jodie. Are you sure you don't mind?"

She laughed softly. "Are you kidding? My kid has a birthday next month. I can take all the extra hours you want to give me."

"You are a lifesaver," Meg assured her. "But don't hesitate to call if you need me."

"Just relax," Jodie insisted. "I've got this."

The call ended, and Meg tucked the cell back into her jeans pocket.

"Problem?"

She turned toward Griff. Now for the next issue. If she couldn't go to work, what should she do?

Spending too much time with this man was not a feasible option.

That would only get her into more trouble, and she was in enough already.

Chapter Four

Meg parked at the medical clinic and walked the block and a half back to her shop. Most of that distance, she kept to the woods behind the alley. Griff had lent her one of his trucks. He had several vehicles that sported the logo for Sundown Farms. Her own truck carried the Pampered Paws one, too easy for the reporters to spot.

It would have been better to avoid coming back for a few hours more, but she really could not stay with Griff any longer. At least not without the risk of crossing a line she did not need to cross. She'd learned to keep their alone time to small windows. Besides, Jodie and Dottie had finished for the day, and the boarded animals had been picked up. Meg could sequester herself to the second floor and just stay stashed away at least until tomorrow.

Sadly, three news vans were still parked in front of her shop, taking up customer parking. Except that it was Sunday and the shop was closed. No doubt at least one of the three would hang around for a long while despite Jodie and Dottie having left and no one else being inside—at least to their knowledge. The upside was that eventually all would give up and go away.

Keeping a close watch on the far end of the alley as well as the corner of her shop, Meg eased through the back gate and into the doggie playground. When she reached the back entrance of her shop, she waited for a while and just listened. The street was quiet at this hour since folks who lived in Piney Woods were either at home or church or gathering at the diner, which was open seven days a week. Some would be lunching or shopping in Chattanooga. The vague sound of chatter from the reporters apparently still hanging out on the sidewalk in front of her shop kept Meg on her toes.

She slipped her key into the lock, gave it a twist and hurried inside. She closed the door, disarmed the security system and locked the door once more. Again, she waited and listened. All quiet. Rather than risk having a look out front, she hustled up the back stairs. They were narrower and steeper, but they were perfect for a moment like this. There was a door at the bottom and at the top. Most people assumed the one on the first floor led to a closet or another room. When she opened the upper door, Raymond lifted his head and stared at her.

He lay at the top of the stairs, where he waited whenever she was away. From that vantage point, he could see her if she came up the main steps or the back ones. She was surprised he wasn't still hanging near Pepper.

Meg squatted and held out her hand, and the old fellow got up and came over to greet her. She gave him a few rubs and a hug. "Hey, boy." She smiled down at the animal to which she had grown far too attached. "We have things to do."

Meg surveyed the studio where she had grown to feel at home. When she'd landed in Piney Woods, she really hadn't expected to feel that way—so *at home*. Growing up an only child and then losing both her parents by the time she was thirty, she hadn't expected to feel at home anywhere—not even in the place she'd lived since leaving for college sixteen years ago. She'd been comfortable in Los Angeles, but she'd never felt that same sort of hominess she'd felt in Bakersfield.

Funny how she'd ignored the idea for all those years.

When her mother had died, at least she'd still had her father. Then, just before her thirtieth birthday, her father's heart attack had changed everything. The farm in Bakersfield had felt like a foreign land. She and her on-again-off-again boyfriend had parted ways. Her place in Los Angeles had felt like…a motel room—not that it ever really felt like home. A place to sleep and shower. Nothing more.

For two and a half years, she had existed in that numbing place. She'd worked and that was about it. Work had consumed her existence. Her tolerance for risk-taking had expanded into territory that more and more resembled carelessness, indifference. Her colleagues had noticed. She'd been warned more than once that she was dancing on an edge.

The warnings and the close calls hadn't changed one thing.

And then came the final act—the end of her story as she knew it.

Meg pushed the thoughts aside. She'd done what she had to do. No going back now.

She opened the bottom drawer of the dresser where most of her clothes were stored. There wasn't really a closet. Anything she wanted hanging did so from the three hooks she'd added to the wall. She removed the layer of socks and undershirts and lifted the false bottom she'd added.

Meg stared at the items she'd hidden there. A passport and driver's license with another name—one she'd hoped not to ever have to use. Stacks of money for emergencies. Keys to the car she kept in a storage unit in town. And the key to the safety deposit box that contained the only proof of the whole truth—not that the truth would ever save her.

"You are beyond saving," she muttered.

Raymond whimpered and eased closer to her. He sensed her distress. She hugged him and scratched him behind the ears. "Don't worry, boy. I'll make sure you and Pepper are taken care of."

Meg thought of Griff. He would take care of them. She didn't even have to ask.

She rounded up a backpack, threw in a couple of changes of underthings and an extra tee. She added the cash she kept on hand and the other items from her hidden compartment to the bottom of the bag.

"Just in case." It was always better to be safe than sorry.

Moving with caution, she eased toward the front

window and checked the street below. All but one of the news vans had left.

Good.

All she had to do was wait out the last one.

Until then, she did a final recon of her place. Made sure she hadn't left anything incriminating. Not much she could do about the fingerprints and DNA. By the time anyone had analyzed all that, she would be long gone. The downside to having to take that step was that everyone she'd come to view as friends would then know she wasn't who she'd said she was. She supposed that was better than just disappearing and leaving them to wonder.

Who was she kidding? The only person whose opinion mattered was Griff. She really hated the idea of him thinking badly of her. But that was inevitable at some point. Even if this whole business blew over without her being outed, he would continue to pursue a closer relationship, and she couldn't allow that to happen. Eventually, he would grow tired of the effort and move on.

An ache pierced her. She closed her eyes and shook her head at the ridiculous reaction. How had she gotten so sloppy over the past twelve months or so?

Her parents had always warned that her internal clock would catch up to her. She hadn't believed them. She had been all about her career. Work had become her life. Sex was just a perk—not something she intended to allow to guide her existence.

As for kids, that was never going to happen. She could never ever put another human being in the line of fire. It was bad enough that she'd allowed Ray-

mond to get attached to this life. But he would learn
to be happy with Griff. The real trouble was with her
learning to be happy *without* Griff.

Meg rolled her eyes. Though they had never even so
much as kissed, she felt closer to him than any other
man in her whole life—besides her dad, anyway. But
that had been a whole different sort of connection.
This thing with Griff was…

"Don't go there." Meg set her backpack next to the
door that led down the backstairs.

Dissecting this thing she felt for Griff would be
like poking needles in her eyes. Whatever *this* was, it
was irrelevant. If she intended to stay alive and protect the people in her wake, she had to keep her head
on straight.

One last pass through her desk, and she was satis-
fied she hadn't overlooked anything. She placed a letter for Jodie on top of her desk. Inside was the deed to
the property and the title to her truck. Both of which
Meg had signed over to her. Jodie was a young single
mom and she had no one. Her parents were junkies
who cared only about their next fix. Jodie was a good
person. This place would give her a future she might
otherwise have difficulty achieving.

Meg hadn't forgotten Dottie either. Dottie was
a retired school teacher who simply loved animals.
She had an adoring family and grown kids who were
there for her. Dottie was set. Still, Meg appreciated
her friendship, and she'd left her a tidy bonus for being
a good friend. She'd always talked about wanting to
take a cruise with her husband but refused to spend the

money. The bonus would take care of several cruises without Dottie having to dip into her savings.

These things Meg left handy just in case. As long as she didn't have to disappear, she would put the items back into her hiding place until that status changed.

Meg made a clicking sound and motioned for Raymond to follow her. She needed to check on Pepper. Jodie would have fed her and let her outside for a while. But if Meg had to disappear, she didn't want to leave without saying goodbye to Pepper.

If she was really lucky all these preparations would be for naught. The next few days would pass, and the story would be forgotten by all but Jennifer and her family. Some other event would top the news, and Meg would just be a distant memory for any interested reporters.

But she couldn't risk not being prepared.

Preparation was the key to survival.

Pepper stood at the door to her kennel. She actually looked better today.

"Hey, girl." Meg opened the kennel and sat down on the floor. Raymond took a position next to her. Damn, she was going to miss this dog.

Pepper joined them, laying her head on Meg's lap. The three of them sat huddled together for a long while. Meg really didn't know how long. She opted not to look at her phone. Instead, she leaned against the wall and allowed her eyes to shutter. She had barely slept last night.

Her eyes drifted closed, and her mind wandered to the farm in Bakersfield, where she ran through the orchard. The air felt cool on her cheeks and her laughter echoed off the trees. She hadn't been home in so long…

Griffin Residence
Sundown Road
2:30 p.m.

DUST ROILING IN the distance had Griff putting a hand over his eyes to see who was headed toward his place. The driveway was a long one, and anyone who'd gotten that far from the road was no doubt looking for him. Either that or they were lost.

Then he spotted the markings on the truck: Sheriff's Department. His pulse quickened. He hoped nothing new had come up with last night's trouble. Instinctively, he checked his cell to ensure he hadn't missed a call or text from Meg.

The truck pulled to a stop in front of his house, and he recognized the driver. Ernie.

Griff relaxed a little. He threw up a hand as he waited for Ernie to emerge from the vehicle and head his way.

"Afternoon," Griff said. "I'm afraid you're too late for lunch." He patted his stomach. "That peanut butter sandwich is long gone."

Ernie laughed. The two of them used to live on peanut butter sandwiches in the summer. Griff's mother warned they were going to go nutty if they didn't learn to like some other lunch besides those sandwiches. She'd finally persuaded them to add bananas. They had laughed and teased his mom that now they were going bananas. She had pretended not to be amused, but he'd seen her secret smiles.

"I could go for a cup of coffee," Ernie said with a grin. "I had lunch at the diner, and it was way better than a peanut butter sandwich."

"Lucky you." Griff hitched his head toward the house. "Come on in." He glanced at the laptop his friend carried. "What's with that?"

"Something I need to show you."

Maybe it was Griff's imagination, but his friend's face blanked and his tone turned serious. Whatever was up didn't seem to be good.

While Griff started a pot of coffee, Ernie settled at the kitchen table and placed the computer on its surface. One hand rested on the device as if he feared it might run off or vanish. He talked about the weather and the blind date he had agreed to on Saturday. Griff laughed and nodded at the right times, but nothing about this felt right.

When the coffee was brewed and cups were filled, Griff joined him at the table. "So, what's up?"

"I'm sure you've spoken with Meg about what happened last night."

"I did." Ernie was aware Griff had a thing for Meg. Ernie had been divorced for two years. He and Griff often discussed their relationship woes.

"How did she seem?" Ernie shrugged. "I mean, was she upset? Calm? What's your take on her reaction?"

Griff's unease escalated. "What's going on, Ernie? We've known each other for a long time. What's with the beating around the bush? If you've got something to say or to ask me, then just do it."

Ernie set his mug aside. "Something's off with Meg. I know how you feel about her and that the two of you are close, but I just have this bad feeling that there's something I'm missing."

Griff digested the words. "Okay. I saw her for a few minutes last night, and we had breakfast together this morning. She stayed awhile to avoid going back to her shop. A couple of reporters were hanging around." He shrugged. "She seemed fine. Last night she was a little shaken, but she was handling it well."

"That's the thing," Ernie said. "She's handling it really well. Even right after it happened, she was as calm as a cucumber. She'd just killed a man, and I would have expected her to be, at the very least, shaken up."

A hint of anger mingled with Griff's uneasiness. "What does that mean?"

Ernie held up both hands. "I'm not accusing her of anything, it's just odd. That's all I'm saying." He exhaled a big breath. "Look, we're like brothers, man. I'm just worried. There's something off, and I can't pretend I didn't pick up on it. I hardly slept last night for mulling this over. It just won't sit right with me, and my gut kept telling me that I needed to talk to you about it."

Griff felt a little irritated. "I've known Meg for about a year, and I've never seen her overreact to anything. Maybe she's just not the type that lets all her emotions show." He had to admit that being forced to kill someone to protect yourself was a big deal, but still, if hiding her emotions was her way, then it was possible...

Ernie just listened and said nothing, but his face told Griff the tale. This was not good.

Hell, Griff didn't understand how to excuse this, whatever it was. What he did get was that his friend was worried. Griff had known Ernie his whole life; if he had a bad feeling about this, it wasn't just his imagination.

"Explain it to me," Griff prompted.

"I wouldn't generally do this," Ernie said as he opened the laptop. "But I think this video explains it better than anything I can say."

"What is this?" Griff studied the screen, recognizing the inside of the Gas and Go.

"This is the video footage from the store's security cameras." Ernie looked straight at him. "It's a clip of what happened between Meg and the dead guy— Zyair Jones."

Griff nodded. "All right. Let's see it."

"I'm going to play it in slow motion. Otherwise you'll miss the things I need you to see, because it happens really fast."

Griff nodded. Ernie pressed Play and the video started.

The clarity wasn't the best, but it was good enough to see the intent on the guy's face. Gun in hand, he was walking toward the checkout counter, prepared to do whatever was necessary. The camera view showed Meg huddled at the end of the counter. Griff's chest constricted.

A scream echoed in the video.

Jones looked over his shoulder toward the back of the place.

Meg had moved ever so slightly to see what he was doing. Suddenly she sprang upward.

Jones turned back toward her.

She was already moving through the air like a ballet dancer. The knife she held sliced across the man's throat even as her body started to turn in midair.

Blood spurted.

The gun fired.

Meg hit the floor, right shoulder first.

Jones staggered, then crumpled to the floor.

Meg got up. She kicked the weapon away, and then, staring at the man, she backed a couple of steps away. The next instant, she turned toward the back of the store and started in that direction.

"That's pretty much what she told me happened," Griff said. His gut was in about fifty knots, and drawing in a breath was as difficult as hell. None of this he intended to let his friend know. His mind kept replaying that twirl, slice and dive maneuver.

Ernie nodded. "Same story she told me."

Griff studied the image on the screen of the paused video that showed Jones face down on the floor in a pool of his own blood and Meg midstride as she walked away. He looked to his friend. "So, what's the problem?"

Ernie scrubbed a hand over his jaw. "There are a couple of things. First, she kicked the gun away."

Griff shrugged. "Smart move. The guy could have grabbed for it as she walked away. If he wasn't dead, I mean."

"Except," Ernie countered, "she didn't appear concerned about him being able to do that since she didn't check to see if she'd completely disabled him. She didn't nudge him, check for a pulse, nothing. She just kicked the gun away from his reach and walked away. Like she knew for sure he was done."

Griff blinked. "Are you suggesting she didn't care that she'd killed this guy?" What the hell was he saying here?

Ernie held up his hands again to show he wasn't here for a fight. "I'm saying she understood that he was dead. She didn't need to check because she recognized the fact by the amount of blood or simply because of the blow she had landed."

Griff shook his head. "Okay, so then what's the problem?"

"There are two problems in my opinion. One," Ernie said, "she killed the guy—obviously in self-defense—and had no visible issue with having done so. I guess what I'm saying is if you had just killed a guy, wouldn't you have some sort of reaction?"

"I can see how it looks that way," Griff agreed, not wanting to sound as if he was talking against Meg. "But that doesn't mean she didn't have an issue. What we're looking at could be shock."

"Maybe," Ernie relented, frowning as if he hadn't considered that possibility.

"What's the other problem?" Griff couldn't keep the frustration out of his voice.

Ernie backed the video up just a little and let it play again, showing the part where she kicked the gun and headed toward the storeroom. "She kicked the gun without stopping to consider what to do with or about it. She just kicked it away." He pointed to the screen. "That was instinct. The kind of thing you do without thinking because you've done it a bunch of times before."

Confusion furrowed Griff's brow and signaled a distant headache there. "You saying she's an ex-cop?"

It was possible. She'd told Griff that she'd had a grooming service in Arizona before her father died and she'd decided on a change of venue. Maybe she had been a cop, and she just didn't want to talk about it.

"I'm saying," Ernie said slowly, "that she was either a cop or…or that she has killed before—" he held up his hands again before Griff could light into him "—and is familiar with the routine of doing the job."

"What the hell, Ernie?" Griff leaned back in his chair and stared at his lifelong friend. "You're suggesting she was not just some sort of killer—but one who had done it enough times to form habits, like kicking a weapon away. Like she was some serial killer or whatever, is that what you're saying?"

"You're taking me all wrong," Ernie argued. "I'm not saying she's a serial killer or something." He rolled his eyes. "My money is on cop."

Either way, worry nudged Griff at the idea. "Play it again."

Ernie started the clip over, once more in slow motion. This time, Griff focused on Meg's face. What he saw was focus, intent. What he did not see was fear or uncertainty.

Whether Meg was a cop or a killer, she had—without question—done this before.

The knots in his gut turned to stone.

But how was that possible? A hurricane of emotions whipped through him. He knew this woman. Had spent hours and hours with her. She loved animals. She loved life. She was one of the nicest people he'd ever met.

"One more time," Griff said, his words barely a whisper.

He had to be missing something. This could not be what it looked like.

Chapter Five

Pampered Paws
Pine Boulevard
3:00 p.m.

Meg jerked awake.

Raymond and Pepper had alerted. Heads up, bodies tense.

On alert herself now, Meg eased to her feet. Listened intently.

Banging on the front entrance made her flinch.

Since it was Sunday and the shop was closed, it wouldn't be a customer. More reporters, she figured. Banging on the door was not acceptable. She'd just have to call Deputy Battles.

Muffled shouting and cursing echoed through the wall that separated her position from the lobby.

Maybe not reporters.

"Come on," Meg murmured to Raymond, ushering him into the open kennel. Pepper followed without prompting. Meg closed the door, careful not to make a sound. If trouble was here, and obviously it was, she didn't want the two elderly dogs getting caught in the fray.

Her first instinct was to call 911, but a part of her worried that if this was the trouble from her past, she feared that she'd only get someone killed. She didn't want Deputy Battles's blood on her hands. If her photo and last night's holdup at the Gas and Go had somehow hit social media or the internet news…

She shook off the idea. Didn't want to go there yet. Instead, she eased forward, all the way to the door that stood between this room and the lobby. Dropping into a crouch, she peered through the keyhole in the old-fashioned door. She'd never felt the need for a key to lock up between the kennels and the lobby. Maybe she should have. A little late now.

Glass shattered.

As she watched through that keyhole, a man's hairy arm reached through the now broken front entrance door and flipped the dead bolt. Her muscles steeled for battle.

Damn. She should have set the security system. She hadn't meant to fall asleep.

One man, then another entered the lobby. The larger guy—tall, thickly muscled—was older, fiftyish. The other was a few inches shorter and a good deal thinner and maybe in his midtwenties. Both wore jeans, tees and biker boots.

A memory of the guy who'd bled out on the floor at the Gas and Go flashed in her brain. Jeans, tee and biker boots.

No doubt these were his friends.

Damn. Just when she thought her biggest worry was Griff's opinion of her.

"Come on out!" the older man shouted. "Don't make us have to hunt you down."

Using a bat, or maybe it was a club he carried, the skinnier guy swiped most of the items on the check-out counter off for emphasis. Thankfully, the vintage cash register teetered near the edge without crashing to the floor. Meg didn't see any firearms, but that didn't mean one or both wasn't carrying. The bigger guy had a sheathed knife, the sort a hunter carried, on his belt. The feel of cool leather at the small of her back was reassuring.

"You got to the count of three," Big Guy warned, "then we're taking this place apart."

No need to let things get out of hand, she decided. Besides, now that it was clear the trouble wasn't what she'd feared, she could handle things. Hopefully without too much fanfare. Just to be sure she didn't have to take this too far, she sent a text message to 911. Maybe no one would have to die before the police arrived. With that out of the way, she tucked her cell back into her pocket and did what she had to do.

She opened the door and walked into the lobby, closing the door firmly behind her.

"Can I help you, gentlemen?" She looked from the older guy to his friend and then to the mess on the floor. Shattered glass and the items that had been on the counter. Nothing irreplaceable. Just a nuisance.

Big Guy glared at her. "You killed my son."

So this was Zyair Jones's father. Regret pricked her. "I'm sorry for your loss, sir. But he didn't leave me a lot of choice. He had a gun pointed at me."

"You mean like this?" Skinny Guy tossed his bat/ club down and drew a weapon.

Meg glanced at him. Nine millimeter. *Damn.* She had hoped neither one was carrying. Oh well, just made things more interesting. The fact that he held the weapon sideways told her he didn't have a freaking clue what he was doing. Just trying to look tough like the thugs in the movies. Did that mean he wouldn't shoot her and, with sheer luck, hit her? She wasn't taking the risk.

Before she could respond, Big Guy growled, "Put that away. I told you I'm doing her the same way she did Zy."

As he spoke, he whipped the knife from its sheath. "Let's see how you like bleeding out alone on the floor."

Meg stared directly into his eyes. "Your son robbed the Gas and Go and was in the process of sexually assaulting the girl who worked there. When I interrupted his criminal activity, he aimed a loaded weapon at me and appeared intent on using it. What would you have done?"

Renewed fury twisted his face. "You think that makes me feel any better? You." He took a step toward her. "Killed." Another step disappeared between them. "My." One more step closer. "Son."

She held his gaze, gave a single nod. "I did. And I guess I'm going to have to kill you too."

While the shock of her daring words startled him, she sack-tapped him with enough force to send him doubling over. The howl of pain that erupted from his mouth echoed through the lobby. She grabbed the vintage cash register—the one thing that remained on the counter—and crashed it against the back of his head. The register hit the floor, and using all of her weight, she shoved the addled man backward.

Skinny Guy jumped astraddle of his downed friend—maybe to protect him, maybe because he was just reckless like that—and waved his weapon. Aiming sideways again. "You are dead, bitch."

Apparently regaining his bearing, Big Guy suddenly lurched upward.

Meg dove for the floor.

Skinny Guy flew forward, and his weapon discharged.

Meg scrambled around to the front of the counter. She grabbed the abandoned bat and shot to her feet just as Big Guy turned toward her. She swung the bat at his head with all her might.

The impact of the hard wood against his skull vibrated up her arms.

He stared at her a moment, his nose gushing blood, his eyes unfocused, then he dropped onto his back. The floor shook with the impact.

A scream rent the air and Skinny Guy threw himself at her.

They tumbled to the floor.

Where was his weapon? Her frantic gaze zoomed from his right hand to his left.

No weapon.

She rolled. Got on top of him.

His hands went to her throat and squeezed.

She punched him in the throat.

His hands dropped immediately to his neck as he gagged and fought for breath.

Rubbing her hand, Meg got up and backed away from the guy now curled into the fetal position.

The sound of sirens in the distance had her breathing a sigh of relief. She went to where the nine millimeter laid on the floor. She picked it up and removed the magazine. Once she confirmed the chamber was clear, she placed the weapon on the counter. One by one, she removed the rounds from the magazine and tossed them over the counter. When she was done, she hurried back to the kennels to ensure Raymond and Pepper were okay. Both stared up at her with worried eyes.

"Good dogs," she murmured, reassuring them before rushing back to the lobby.

The sheriff's department SUV squealed to a rocking stop outside her shop. Two deputies, including Ernie Battles, barreled through the door, weapons drawn. Both surveyed the damage and the wounded.

Battles turned to Meg. "You okay?"

She nodded. Shook her right hand. "I'm good."

The Big Guy roused and scrambled to his hands and knees. Then he puked.

Battles nudged the man with his weapon. "Mr. Jones, you are under arrest…"

The rest of what the deputy said was lost on Meg. Her attention had zeroed in on the reporter with her face pressed to the glass. Worse, her cameraman stood in the open entrance, filming the whole thing.

Holy…

"Back off," the other deputy warned as he moved

toward the doorway. "This is a crime scene. I need you back on the street."

The reporter shouted Meg's name.

She turned her back.

"How does it feel to know you killed a man?" The words echoed through the air.

Meg glanced toward the woman being ushered off the sidewalk and back to her van. Two more news vans arrived while she watched.

Dread welling inside her, Meg walked to the counter and sat down on the floor behind it.

Whatever privacy she had hoped to keep intact after all this was gone now. Her face and this new story would be all over the internet by tomorrow. Any hope of maintaining anonymity was gone.

The jig was up.

Two other deputies arrived and hauled the perps away in separate cruisers. By then, Battles had taken Meg's statement and she had started the cleanup. The other deputy, Hershel Gardner, had rounded up a box from the dumpster in the alley and was helping with the glass pickup.

The best part of this, Meg decided—looking on the bright side—was that it had occurred late in the day. No way would it hit the news before morning. The minutes that had elapsed also had her thinking that if she was really lucky, the story wouldn't get picked up by a big network or the Associated Press. No reason for it to, in her opinion. There was plenty of bad going on in the world to keep her issues way down at the bottom on the interest barrel.

"Can we talk?" Battles asked.

"Sure." Meg propped the broom she'd been using against the wall and followed the deputy over to the counter.

Battles searched her face before saying whatever was on his mind. Meg hoped he wasn't going to ask more questions about her self-defense techniques.

"I need you to rethink this thing about not wanting to press charges," he suggested. "I get that you feel bad for Mr. Jones because his son is dead, but you did what you had to do. It was self-defense. Jones has to get right with that. To be honest with you, he's likely part of the reason his son was always in trouble. If Jones gets away with this, it just gives him more power."

Meg understood what he was saying—better than most probably—but she also understood that Jones had been operating on emotion. "The breaking and entering should stand," she agreed. "But not the assault. I think he already got the short end of the stick on that one."

"No question," Battles granted. "But what about the next person he gets riled up at? Will that person be able to fend him off the way you did? If he gets away with what he did to you, then down the road, someone else may end up paying the price."

He had a valid point. Maybe too valid. Meg should have thought of that. Maybe she was operating on emotion a little too fully as well.

"You're right. He should face the full ramifications for what he did, and maybe he won't be so bold next time."

Battles nodded. "Good." He chuckled. "You know, I'm still trying to figure out how you handled a guy at least three times your size. Not to mention he had an accomplice with him who was armed."

She laughed. "I think what really helped was the element of surprise. They didn't see the potential for a real fight."

Battles shrugged. "Maybe so. But the way you emptied that magazine on the weapon and…" He shrugged again. "I don't know, just the way you handle yourself reminds me of my own training."

"Maybe I watch too many cop shows. Picked up on some of the moves. You know how television and social media can influence our thoughts and actions."

He nodded slowly. "Yeah, I guess you're right."

Voices outside drew their attention to the street. The first reporter was gone. Had to get her story in before anyone else, no doubt. The other two were shouting questions at a new arrival.

Griff.

Meg's heart reacted and she silently chastised herself.

He climbed out of his truck, then reached into the back for what appeared to be a sheet of plywood.

"I should give him a hand," Battles said.

The deputy hustled outside and helped Griff bring in the four-by-eight sheet of plywood. Once they'd propped it against the wall, Griff glanced at her before going back outside. Meg blinked, considering if she should have said something.

While Battles ushered the two reporters and their cameramen off the sidewalk and back to the street—again—Griff returned carrying a toolbox. This time, he walked all the way back to where she stood.

"Hey."

She sighed. "Hey."

"We're going to secure your front entrance," he explained. "Then I'm coming around back to pick up you and Raymond. You should pack a bag. I plan on keeping you for a while."

"But—"

He shook his head. "No buts. Jodie and Dottie can take care of things around here. You need to disappear for a few days until the smoke clears."

He was right. She understood this. The problem was he didn't, not really. For now, this was her only real option. "Okay."

She climbed the stairs, the receding adrenaline making her feel as if she'd run a triathlon. Since she'd already packed her go bag, all she needed was another with a couple changes of clothes and a nightshirt. Well, and her toothbrush and hairbrush. A few toiletries. She could hang out at Griff's for a couple of days and see how this was going to shake down. Maybe she'd get lucky, and the story would go unnoticed. After all, small-town Tennessee was a long way from big-city California.

She could hope anyway.

Truth was, she probably wouldn't feel safe going forward, whether the story made headlines or not. The life she lived was uncertain enough without layering in the extra issue of not one but two very public situations.

If she dared to stay, how would she ever stop looking over her shoulder after all this?

Staying was a less than optimal idea. But going

filled her with a kind of sadness she'd never expected to feel again.

She had allowed herself to get far too close to this place. She walked to her beloved window and watched Griff get something from the back of his truck and head back into her shop. She was way too close to this man.

It was dangerous, too dangerous.

There was no guarantee she could protect him if her past caught up with her.

Chapter Six

Despite all that had happened, Meg smiled when the truck rolled to a stop at the end of Griff's long driveway. The herd of dogs that had been lying on the porch all stood, ears perked up, tails cautiously wagging.

As soon as Griff opened his door and the dogs got his scent, they were yapping and rushing toward him. It was the closest thing to heaven she could imagine in this life.

Meg parked her truck next to his and climbed out. What was not to like about a man who loved dogs—animals in general—this much? More telling was the fact that the animals clearly loved him. That they had a haven here was just icing on the cake.

He joined her at her truck and grabbed her overnight bag. "You mind if I get this bunch fed before we make dinner?"

She picked up her backpack from the floorboard. "As long as you don't mind if I help."

He grinned and reached for the backpack. "I never turn down a helping hand."

Meg opened the back door and helped Pepper from the back seat. Raymond managed to hop down all on his own. The two followed her to the front of his truck where they waited while Griff took her bags into the house. He hadn't been too happy about her insisting on driving herself over here, but she couldn't imagine being stranded in the event she had to leave. An exit strategy was far too important to be caught with no wheels.

When he went into the house she noticed he hadn't locked his door. Not a good idea, especially with her around. She'd have to talk to him about that. Or maybe she'd do him a big favor and disappear. It would be in his best interest.

The way her gut clenched made her regret having been so foolish. She should never have allowed herself to get so comfortable here, to believe for one second that she might be able to have a real fresh start the first time around. The move and then the acceptance of people in this town had been far too simple. She should have known it was too good to be true.

The herd, as Griff called them, followed him down the steps. A few low growls were exchanged as they eyed Pepper and Raymond, but Griff gave the command for the group to behave and the growls stopped. The animals, including the interlopers belonging to Meg, followed Griff and her to what looked like a barn but was actually a very large state-of-the-art doghouse. Dozens of kennels and all else that his herd might need was inside. He called each dog by name as they portioned food into their bowls.

"Pepper," Griff said as he opened the door to a vacant kennel, "I was thinking you might like this one."

Pepper sniffed the door, then wandered into the kennel and over to the bowl of kibble.

Griff closed the door. "Raymond, you come on with us."

Griff was aware that Raymond slept at Meg's bedside, and though none of his many animals stayed in the house with him, he'd insisted he wouldn't mind Raymond doing so. The sweet Lab he'd had for fourteen years had died last year, and so far Griff wasn't ready for another one to get that close. Meg understood. It was like losing a family member.

Once the dogs were settled, they moved on to the "cat barn." The four-legged furry animals seemed to come out of the woodwork. Raymond stuck close to Meg. Though he was around cats at the shop, never so many at one time.

The cat barn had once been a smokehouse used by Griff's grandparents for curing meat before the common availability of freezers. Inside were all manner of climbing areas that led to cozy little nooks. A total of fifteen cats pranced about, taking a turn at rubbing against Griff's legs. They too adored him.

Once the cats were served, Griff and Meg moved on to the big original barn where they fed the eight horses and four cows. There were two large pigs rooting around in a smaller pasture beyond the barn, and they got a little something as well. Raymond was quite curious about the snorting creatures. Meg was fairly certain he'd been around horses and cows before but never pigs.

As they headed to the house, Meg surveyed Griff's farm. No matter how many times she came here, she was still impressed by the well-thought-out setup and the enduring relationship between Griff and the animals. It really was a special place. She glanced at the man next to her. A special man.

Who deserved a woman without secrets, who could share this wonderful life with him.

She blinked away the notion. Certainly not her.

Inside, he picked up her bags and said, "I'll take these upstairs."

She nodded and did what she knew needed to be done. "I'd feel more comfortable if we locked the doors."

He studied her a moment, then gave a quick nod of his own. "Course."

She locked the door and he headed up. She moved on to the kitchen and locked the back door as well. The urge to search the house gnawed at her, but she ignored it. There was no reason for her to suspect an ambush at his address. At least not yet.

Sad. Very sad.

He joined her in the kitchen. "Your room is the second door on the right upstairs. There's only one bathroom up there. I hope you don't mind sharing."

"Not at all. I'm grateful for your hospitality."

He waved her off and headed for the fridge. "Rhianna Glen dropped off a casserole this afternoon." He withdrew a white covered dish embossed with pink flowers. "Chicken, broccoli and rice, I think she said."

Meg grinned. "I see. Rhianna Glen, huh? That's nice." No matter that she kept a teasing lilt in her voice, jealousy poked at her. This was the sort of woman who would end up wrangling Griff. Someone who had no secret past, someone who had the option of staying forever.

He laughed as he set the dish on the counter, removed the lid and prepared to put it in the microwave. "She's just trying to be nice."

Now Meg laughed outright. "I know you aren't that naive. She's recently divorced and you are a very…" How did she put it without sounding overly interested? "A good catch."

He pressed the Start button and the microwave hummed to life. "Good catch." His forehead furrowed and he executed a slow nod. "Makes me feel kind of like a largemouth bass."

Meg barely suppressed another round of laughter. "You know what I mean. Rhianna is a woman of a certain age whose upbringing has taught her that having a husband is the only way to be happy, and therefore, she must replace the old model posthaste."

Now Griff was the one laughing. "I guess so. Plenty of that going around lately."

Meg leaned against the counter next to the sink. "So, you're saying Rhianna isn't the only one."

Rhianna and her husband had divorced after four short years. No children. Rhianna was a lifetime resident of Piney Woods. She no doubt felt she should have first dibs on the town's most eligible bachelor.

He shrugged, reached into the cupboard for plates.

"There may be a couple of others who bring me food. It's nothing new."

Meg decided she wouldn't mention people did that for funerals too. "They say the stomach is the way to a man's heart."

He placed the plates on the counter next to her. "Not this man."

He held her gaze for several seconds, and the look in his eyes somehow prevented her from breathing. "Sorry," she said in the lightest tone she could muster. "I wasn't aware you liked casseroles so much."

"I don't…really." He searched her face as if looking for answers to something he wanted to ask.

Uh-oh. Back to the questions. She shifted away, opened the utensil drawer and grabbed a couple of forks. "It sure smells good." He said nothing but it was true. "I've never been much of a cook," she rambled on. She'd tried since getting settled in Piney Woods, but her heart had never been in it.

When she turned back to him and passed the forks, he said, "Clearly you have other skills."

His gaze held hers in that probing way again, and somehow, try as she might, she couldn't look away. "Most animals love me, so I guess that's my super-power."

"That's not what I meant." He laid the forks on the plates without taking his eyes off hers. "How in the world did you disable two men all by yourself?"

"I told you about the self-defense classes." Was it her imagination, or was he standing purposefully closer, searching her eyes a little more intently?

He moved his head slowly side to side. "This was

more than self-defense classes. Ernie says you put both down without a weapon. That one guy was huge. I couldn't have put him down. Not without some sort of advantage." His eyes narrowed. "What kind of advantage did you have?"

"The cash register," she said, struggling to prod answers from her brain. She'd foolishly lapsed into some trancelike state prompted by nothing more than Griff's nearness and his eyes. "I slammed it over his head after I kicked him…well, you know where."

Griff winced. "And what was the other guy doing during all this?"

"Watching, I think." She allowed the events to play out in her head. "He waved his gun at me, but the big guy got up and knocked him over. It was a total accident but really worked to my advantage."

This time Griff frowned. "I'm not following."

"When the big guy first went down, the skinny guy jumped to stand over him." She shrugged. "I don't know, maybe it was some sort of couldn't-get-it-right ninja move to protect his friend and at the same time confront me. Then things got a little chaotic. I dove for the floor. The gun went off." She shrugged. "I found the bat the skinny one had brought in with him and used it on the big guy. He went down again. But the skinny guy jumped up." She rubbed her forehead, trying to recall the precise chain of events. "Next thing I knew, he had me by the throat and I punched him in his throat." She looked at her right hand. Her knuckles were swollen and her fingers were a little blue. "Hurt like hell, but it hurt him worse."

Griff took her hand in his and rubbed his fingers over hers. "You need something for that?"

She watched his fingers on hers, savored the feel of her hand in his. "It's okay. I've suffered worse, believe—" She caught herself too late, squeezed her eyes shut for a second. "I mean, I was in an accident once and broke my arm. That hurt a whole lot worse. I've had a…"

He was watching her so intently that she couldn't continue speaking. She wanted to, told herself to, but the words would not come.

"It feels like there are things you need to tell me," he said softly. "Things that are relevant to how you can take down two men all alone. How you can stop a man carrying a gun with nothing but your wits and a knife."

"Self-defense classes." The lie was sounding weaker all the time.

"You can tell me anything," he said, his gaze pressing hers with an insistence that made her weak. "You know that, right?"

She nodded. "I do. We're friends."

"Then why aren't you telling me?"

The images of him being tied to a chair and tortured then shot loomed in her mind. She drew her hand from his and steadied herself. Not an easy feat.

"You're overthinking this." She manufactured a smile that no doubt looked as fake as it felt. "I just got lucky. Those guys weren't nearly as tough as they work at appearing. The younger guy got all his moves from thug TV, I think."

The microwave dinged, and she had never been so thankful for Rhianna Glen's casserole.

Griff hesitated but then finally turned to take the casserole from the microwave. He placed it on the counter, then tossed the oven mitts aside and searched for a serving spoon.

Meg grabbed a couple of napkins from the holder next to the salt and pepper shakers and placed them on the table. "What're we drinking?"

"I have beer, tea, water," he replied as he placed their plates on the table. "Take your pick."

Though she rarely allowed anything that might alter her ability to think clearly, Meg decided she deserved a beer. Like last night, this had been a hell of a day. "I'll take a beer. How about you?"

"Sounds good," he agreed.

She grabbed the beers from the fridge and settled at the table. For a while, they ate and chatted about the dogs. The casserole was actually very good. They both laughed at the idea that Rhianna likely wouldn't appreciate him sharing her dish with another woman. Then they cleaned up, grabbed another beer and headed into the living room. Meg relaxed a little and decided that maybe he was going to let the whole issue go.

Deputy Battles hadn't really given her much trouble when she gave her statement. No doubt he had been a little shocked by the scene and the fact that she'd been the only one left standing but chose to overlook it, considering the two men had invaded her shop and had done considerable damage. After all, she had been lucky to survive. But time had cleared his head, and judging by the questions Griff had asked, he and Ernie had discussed what went down in her store. The more they talked, the more questions came to mind.

Now, obviously, they were both suspicious. And who wouldn't be? The question was, could she alleviate their concerns?

The ways she might accomplish that goal twisted inside her. Just another reason the life she had built here was in all probability over. Even if her past didn't find her, *this* would haunt her. No one would be able to just feel grateful she'd survived. There would always be questions just because she had come through unscathed, not one but two close calls. It was human nature. People were curious. They needed reasonable explanations and her explanations had not been anywhere near reasonable enough.

The quiet went on for longer than was comfortable. Guilt heaped heavier onto her shoulders and Meg struggled with something to say. She didn't like that her closest friend—and Griff was that and, if she were totally honest, more—was disappointed in her or whatever it was he felt.

But she could not go down that path with him. His life would be changed in ways he couldn't possibly understand, and she refused to be responsible for altering his entire existence to that degree.

Griff set his can aside and turned to her as if he'd finally landed on what he wanted to say next. "Are you concerned those two men will come after you again?" He studied her a moment. "I mean, you did agree without much persuasion to come home with me. I'm guessing you're at least a little worried, whether you want to admit it or not."

Meg chose her words carefully. To tell him that an abrupt exit from his place would likely be simpler and cleaner than from her shop wouldn't be the response he wanted to hear.

"I suppose I was in a sort of shock. The idea that the man's family would seek revenge never even entered my mind. Apparently, it should have." This was frankly an oversight on her part. She wouldn't have made such a rookie error in the past. Maybe she was getting soft.

"Ernie's worried there will be others, even though the two involved in today's attack won't be giving you any trouble anytime soon. Sheriff Norwood is working with the sheriff in Dade County to get a handle on the situation."

Meg nodded. "Good to know."

"Someone could confront you on the road," Griff added. "At the market. It's something you need to give some thought to."

Wait. Wait. She got it now. This was more than just about her. "Is there something about the Jones family that you and Ernie haven't told me?"

"There are a lot of good people out there who belong to very cool, very nice biker clubs. But the Jones folks are not nice, and they don't belong to a club like that. This is a criminal biker gang. Sheriff Norwood mentioned there was an FBI investigation into these guys. We're talking bad guys, Meg. Really, really bad guys."

As if she needed the situation ramped up. The FBI? Really? This just got better and better.

"Okay." She finished off her beer. "This is why

you're so worried?" On some level the news was a
relief. If this was the primary factor troubling Griff,
then maybe he wasn't as suspicious of her as she'd
believed. Somehow that made her feel a little better.
"I just have to watch my back until this is sorted."

"We," he corrected. "We watch your back."

She grinned. Toyed with her empty beer can. "You
may not find the job as interesting as you think."

The ghost of a smile tugged at his lips, but he
wasn't ready to shrug off the seriousness just yet. "I'm
willing to find out."

Again, she carefully selected her words. "You're
a good friend, Griff. I appreciate your consideration
of my welfare."

"I appreciate," he teased, "that you keep my life interesting."

Meg laughed. She wasn't sure if that was a compli-
ment. "I wish I could say I try, but to be honest, the
interesting part just barges in."

"Ernie wondered if you had ever considered keeping a handgun for protection."

If she'd had any other question about the idea, this
was clearly confirmation that they had indeed been
discussing her. "I'm good with my knife."

Handguns, if done legally, involved background
checks. Not doable. If she told him she already had
a weapon, then she'd have to reveal that it had not
been legally purchased. Either way, this would create
a problem. It was best to insist she didn't like guns.
And she didn't. Not really. That said, they were a necessary evil sometimes.

"I have a rifle you could keep at your place."

"I appreciate the offer, but I wouldn't feel comfortable with a rifle."

"We could do some target practice with it tomorrow. Get you comfortable with it." He grinned. "See how bad you really are."

"Couldn't hurt, I suppose." What else could she say? Not that she was an expert marksman. Not that she could disassemble and reassemble any firearm he chose to put in front of her in record time.

"Good. I, for one, will feel better knowing you've got a little firepower handy."

"I'm tired of talking about me," she said, curling her legs under her and settling deeper into the comfy sofa. "Tell me about how you decided to become a keeper of discarded things."

"Didn't we talk about this before?"

"I've asked, and you've always given me the abridged version. I want the details."

He leaned back, draped an arm across the back of the sofa. "I guess I had that one coming."

For the first time since before she'd spotted the holdup at the Gas and Go, she relaxed and waited for him to continue. Just avoiding further discussion about her was a significant boost to lowering her tension.

"I was working sixteen-hour days," he began. "Not that I didn't love my job, but there's a fine line between love and obsession. I think it was easier than coming home and facing the discord there."

"Relationships can be difficult sometimes." Meg was well aware. Her one serious relationship had crumbled under the tension of high-pressure work. Hers and his. Man, that had been so long ago. *Another life.*

"I guess I didn't want to see the end coming, but it came anyway, whether I was here or not. Once it was over, I had to ask myself why I was pouring my whole life into something that should only occupy a small portion of it." He glanced around the room. "I wanted to be here doing something that mattered at least part of my time. One evening, I went out to get my car from the parking garage, and there was a dog. It looked alone and sad, neglected. I gave it a scratch behind the ears and the bag of chips I had in my car." He stared at his hands a moment. "The next evening it was still there. So I loaded him up and took him to a shelter. That was when my eyes were really opened. There just aren't enough shelters—worse, there aren't enough decent humans, in my opinion—to care for the animal population. I decided I had to do something."

"You could have donated funds for building more shelters. That's what most people do. Throw a little money at it. Sometimes it's the best they can do. Sometimes it's just easier that way because you don't have to look too closely."

"I did that too," he said with a pointed look in her direction. "And I still do. But I had all this land, and since farming wasn't my thing, I decided to use it for something that mattered. I can't save the world, but I can do all possible to save the part of it that I live in."

"Wow." She had known part of that story, but this, this was the sort of tale real-life heroes were made of. "That's amazing."

"I still enjoy the work I do on a professional level at the firm, but most of my time is spent here doing what matters."

"I'm sure your mom and your sister are very proud of what you're doing here." How could they not be? This was amazing.

He chuckled. "Mostly, I think they believe I'm in denial about barreling toward forty with no wife and no kids and nary a prospect."

Meg wanted to laugh at the idea, but she got the distinct impression that he was serious. "I'm sure your family would love to hear about your casserole queens."

"I think they'd enjoy hearing about you."

Their gazes held for a long moment. Every ounce of will power Meg possessed was required not to pursue his motive behind the statement.

Instead, she stood, stretched and yawned. "I'm beat. I hope you don't mind if I hit the shower and call it a night a little early."

"Right." He pushed to his feet. "I'm sure you're exhausted. Make yourself at home."

"Thanks." She backed away a step. "See you in the morning." She headed for the stairs.

"Night," he called after her.

"Night," she said without looking back. She couldn't trust herself to look back without running right into his arms.

Chapter Seven

Meg flinched. Shook her head.

The cold touched her again.

She jerked awake.

Raymond sat beside the bed, his muzzle resting on the quilt. Even as her gaze focused in on him, he nudged her with his cold nose again.

Meg laughed and swiped at her eyes. "Morning, boy."

The light filtering in through the window had her frowning. What time was it? She grabbed her cell from the bedside table and sat up. 7:30 a.m.

Her eyebrows reared up. She *never* slept past 5:30 or 6:00 a.m. Ever.

She threw the covers back and bounced out of bed. "Raymond, why didn't you get me up sooner?"

He stared up at her with a questioning look as if to ask how he was supposed to have done that.

"You're right," she agreed as she dug through her overnight bag for clothes, "I should have set the alarm on my phone."

But she usually woke up on her own. Maybe knowing someone else was in the house with her had helped her sleep more deeply. She dragged on her jeans. Not just someone but a friend. A good friend.

She pulled on a tee, finger-combed her hair and pulled it back into a ponytail using the scrunchie she wore as a bracelet whenever it wasn't in her hair. Not just a friend, she admitted. A guy she respected, thought was sexy and was kind of attracted to. Truth was she'd lain in bed for hours last night thinking about him just down the hall. Wondering what it would be like to be in his bed. Wishing she could just enjoy that opportunity and never worry about consequences.

That was the reason she'd overslept. Even at thirty-four, a girl could be kept awake by fantasies.

"Not smart," she muttered, slipping on her favorite sneakers.

She straightened the covers on her bed and hung her nightshirt on the footboard. She folded yesterday's clothes and set them on the bed. Maybe she'd have a chance to launder them later. She didn't have many things with her and she had to stay prepared.

At the door, she opened it wider and peeked out. The hallway was clear. She hurried to the bathroom, freshened up and did necessary business. Then she headed for the stairs. Raymond followed her to the top of the stairs. As they descended the staircase, the scent of coffee had her moving faster. Downstairs, she headed for the kitchen. The smell of toasted bread and maybe bacon had her stomach rumbling. If the man cooked too, she might just have to marry him.

Even the thought had her feeling an odd little jab in the center of her chest.

Not possible.

Approaching the kitchen, she paused and grinned at the scene. An apron was cinched at Griff's waist. He carefully lifted pieces of browned bacon from the pan to a plate lined with a paper towel. The light in the oven showed a tray of biscuits. The man made biscuits? Then he turned to another pan and gave it a stir with a spatula. Eggs? Grease popped and he swore. Meg leaned against the door jamb and folded her arms over her chest to watch.

But Raymond had other ideas. He scooted in around her and gave a single deep-throated bark.

Griff turned around and looked from Raymond to Meg. His face flushed a little. "Morning."

"Were you just going to let me sleep all day?" She pushed off the door and joined him at the stove.

He shrugged. "I figured you didn't sleep much the last couple of nights and needed a little extra."

A reasonable conclusion. "Thanks." She surveyed the bacon and eggs. "Looks and smells great. What can I do to help?"

He turned off the oven, removed the pan of biscuits and gestured to the table. "Have a seat. It's all done."

"Then it's only fair that I do the cleanup." Meg crossed to the coffee maker and poured herself a cup.

Griff plated the eggs and bacon, then added a biscuit to each. He settled the plates on the table and then rounded up forks and napkins. "You may have noticed I don't have a dishwasher."

"Neither do I." Truth was, she mostly used paper

plates. Not to mention, she ordered from the diner really often. Cooking for one was not so much fun. She took a seat at the table and savored a taste of coffee. So good she moaned. "You make really great coffee."

"I'm glad you like it." He sat down in the seat opposite her. "How about we do the cleanup together, and then I don't have to feel guilty about my guest washing dishes by hand."

She laughed. "I certainly wouldn't want you feeling guilty."

Raymond decided he wasn't getting a treat, so he stretched out on the floor next to Meg's chair.

"Please tell me you didn't make these biscuits from scratch." She bit into the soft, fluffy baked good and moaned again. She might just moan and sigh through this entire meal.

"My mama's recipe."

Meg rolled her eyes. "You put me to shame, Avery Griffin. I couldn't make a biscuit from scratch if my life depended on it."

He chuckled. "I guess I'll just have to teach you."

The suggestion filled her head with all sorts of notions that had nothing to do with baking.

"Speaking of family," he said after a few minutes of devouring the delicious meal, "my sister called this morning. She insists that we come to lunch at her place on Sunday. You have any plans?"

She would so love to say yes, but she couldn't even be sure she'd still be here. Yet, the hope in his voice, in his eyes, had her agreeing. "I do not have plans. I would love to go."

"Great." He dove back into his meal, but not before she noticed the sparkle her answer had put in his eyes.

She really hoped she didn't have to disappoint him.

Determined not to borrow more trouble than she already had, she put all else aside and just enjoyed the moment. It felt good, maybe too good, chatting with Griff over the breakfast he'd made and then washing the dishes together. She imagined this was how it would be if they were together.

Do not go there.

She knew better, but it was impossible not to imagine how it would feel to live this life, this partnership with the two of them working together and laughing and feeling just like a team. What would it hurt to let herself dream for a few minutes?

In her back pocket, her cell vibrated, drawing Meg from the fantasy. She stilled, withdrew it and checked the screen. Long ago—right after she exited her former life—she had set up notifications for anything that appeared online related to who she was previously. For a while, the notifications had come frequently and furiously. She'd topped the headlines on the West Coast for a few months.

Eventually, the notifications had dwindled to nothing. Since moving to Piney Woods, she hadn't received a single one. She was gone, probably dead, and there wasn't a soul on the planet who cared.

But this notification wasn't about the person she used to be. This was about Megan Lewis, owner/operator of Pampered Paws in Piney Woods, Tennessee. This was about her life now.

The one that was, as of this second, officially over.

Her heart sank to her knees.

Her name and, worse, her photo filled the screen. Several news outlets in both Tennessee and Georgia had picked up the story. That was troubling enough, but it was the pickup by the Associated Press that sealed her fate.

No One Messes with This Woman

The story explained how Megan Lewis of Piney Woods, Tennessee, was a hero. Not only had she rescued a young girl from a savage fate, she had taken on the would-be killer's vigilante family, kicking butt and taking names.

Cold seeped into her bones as she read several versions of the same story. Her face appeared over and over—images all credited to the one reporter who'd lingered after yesterday's invasion at Meg's shop.

"You okay?"

Meg blinked. Shoved her phone back into her pocket. "I'm sorry, what?"

Griff had moved in toe-to-toe with her. He searched her face. "You look like you've seen a ghost."

She had. Meg swallowed back the dread rising in her throat. Her own.

"It's nothing." She forced a smile. "What's next on this morning's agenda? I'm guessing there are a lot of animals ready for their breakfast."

She couldn't think. Couldn't kick the voices from her head. *They will see this. They will come. Your life here is over.*

She had to get Griff moving into his day so she could

figure out the best plan for exiting this life, for leaving everything behind. She thought of Raymond, and her heart hurt.

Griff's worry shifted into a grin, somehow dragging her from the painful thoughts. "Mornings are my favorite part of the day."

She forced a smile, hoping he wouldn't see through it. "I can't wait to see what makes you say so."

He led the way to the barn, where they hayed the horses and cows. Added a bucket of feed to the pig trough. Meg struggled with keeping this new reality at bay so that she could enjoy this last morning with Griff and the animals. After the big animals were done, they moved on to the cats and then the dogs, all of which were freed to roam. Griff allowed the cats and dogs free range all day every day. He preferred putting them back into their kennels at night. The animals seemed to feel more comfortable that way, he explained. Maybe because the routine of it felt comforting. Then Meg and Griff gathered a few eggs in the chicken coop and restocked their feeders. She understood exactly why this was the best part of his day.

Meg felt so grateful for having been able to share it with him.

"I should drop Pepper at the vet clinic." She reached down and rubbed Raymond on the head. He'd followed every step they had taken. She suspected he sensed something was wrong. "Is it okay if I leave Raymond here until I get back?"

"Sure. I have some work to do in my office." He grinned at the dog. "Raymond can keep me company."

"Thanks. I'll just get my wallet and keys, then I'll load up Pepper."

He hitched his head toward the house. "You get your stuff. I'll load Pepper into your truck."

"I appreciate it."

Meg walked back to the house, holding back the urge to run. The longer she stayed at this point, the more dangerous for anyone who had been associated with her. Trudging up the stairs, she considered that leaving Griff a note would be a nice gesture, but there was no time to explain. No time to say the things that had swelled into her throat. How did she tell him that all he thought he knew about her was a lie? Whatever suspicions he had about her based on the events of the past two days would never in a million years live up to the truth. The truth was far scarier and far uglier.

Some secrets were better left buried.

Except hers was about to be exhumed in the worst kind of way.

The friends she had foolishly made, the reputation she had built would all be shattered when the truth came out, and it was coming. There was no holding it back at this point. She couldn't stop the hurricane. Her only hope was to try and limit the devastation.

She picked up her backpack. Leaving the overnight bag was necessary so as not to draw suspicion from Griff when she walked out. She descended the stairs and hesitated at the front door. A last, lingering look around and she was gone. Allowing herself to get so attached had been a bad move on her part. She had known better.

Griff waited at the driver side door of her truck.

When she reached him, he opened the door for her. Why did he have to be so nice? So caring? Her entire soul ached. So damned handsome?

"I should drop by the shop," she said, hoping to extend the time she had before he started to wonder why she wasn't back.

"Just be careful," he said. "I called Ernie, and he says there's no one else in the Jones family you need to worry about, but they haven't interviewed all the members of that biker club yet. You need to be careful until we know if the threat is over."

He had no idea.

Meg gave him a little salute. "Yes, sir."

He caught her hand when she lowered it. "It's important to me that you're careful, Meg. To tell you the truth, I'd feel better going with you."

If he hadn't stared into her eyes that way, she might have been able to ignore the way his hand held hers so protectively. "I appreciate that and I promise I'll be careful. You have plenty to do here. I'll be fine."

And then the final nail in her coffin. He leaned down and brushed his lips across hers.

If she had been smart, she would have drawn away, but she simply could not. She wanted more. If she never saw him again after today, at least she would have this one kiss to remember him by.

So not smart.

But oh so sweet.

She melted into him, her backpack hitting the ground and her arms going around his neck. His arms went around her waist and pulled her closer.

The desperation that clawed through her was nearly

more than she could bear, but she had to resist. She would not allow the danger to find her here, where he could be hurt. She had to go. She had to go now. Drawing the trouble away from here—away from him was paramount.

She drew back. Pressed her forehead to his chin because she didn't dare look into his eyes again. She might be strong, but she was not that strong.

"I should get going."

"I wish you didn't have to go."

Her hands slid down to his chest, and she levered herself away. Somehow managed to meet his eyes. "See you later," she lied.

He nodded. "Later."

She picked up her backpack and climbed into her truck. Before pulling out, she waved. He waved back, and then he watched until she was driving away. She watched too as he grew more distant in her rearview mirror.

Gripping the steering wheel as hard as she could, Meg kept going. She glanced over at Pepper and smiled. "Don't worry. Griff will bring you back home after all your tests."

He would take care of Pepper and Raymond.

Meg didn't have to ask or to wonder, she knew he would. That was the kind of man he was.

Dropping Pepper off at the vet clinic was easy enough. She told Lonnie if he couldn't reach her with the test results to call Griff. Lonnie assured her that he would, and Meg headed into town. A truck parked in front of Pampered Paws sported a glass repair logo. She was glad Jodie had found someone who could come so quickly. Meg parked in the alley behind the shop next door. She needed to talk to Jodie—and Dottie too if she was in. She wasn't sure just yet how the conversation would go, but it had to be done. She could simply rely on the letter she'd left, but this way would be better.

The usual crew of dogs were in the back play space. Meg gave individual attention to each of the animals as she made her way to the back door. She entered the code and stepped inside. Pop music played softly. Meg smiled. Jodie was in for sure. Dottie preferred country music. If she was in, she would insist that customers preferred country as well. Jodie never argued with the older woman. Whether it was respect or friendship, she always allowed Dottie to have her way.

Jodie was just outside the newly repaired front entrance and was handing a check to the repairman when Meg entered the lobby. The man thanked Jodie and went on his way. Jodie came inside, closing the door behind her. Her face brightened when she spotted Meg.

"You're here. Everything okay?"

The urge to tell her no and all the reasons it wasn't okay surged into Meg's throat, but she couldn't go there. Now or ever.

"Everything's fine. I dropped Pepper at the vet's. Griff is going to take her in when she's ready to be picked up."

"Aww, that's great. Pepper will love it there. Griff is such a great guy." She waggled her eyebrows as she joined Meg behind the counter. "You know he's really stuck on you. I mean, seriously stuck."

Meg smiled sadly. "He's a great guy for sure."

Jodie rolled her eyes. "Just pretend I didn't say the rest."

Now or never. "There's something I need to show you."

Her friend and employee picked up on the nuance of disquiet in Meg's tone. "What's going on?"

"You know," Meg began, "I don't have any family."

Jodie nodded slowly. "You told me, yes."

"After what happened on Saturday night, I got a little worried about things."

Jodie's face scrunched with worry. "Not to mention those guys busting in here yesterday. That had to be terrifying."

Meg nodded. "A little."

Jodie grinned sheepishly. "But you did kick their butts."

"I did." Meg pushed aside the images that immediately popped into her head. "Anyway, I wanted to make sure you knew about this." She reached into the cash register, lifted the cash tray from the drawer. She set it aside and picked up the unmarked envelope she'd tucked last year. "About six months ago, I started thinking about this, and I decided to do something about it."

Meg opened the envelope and removed the three-page document. She handed it to Jodie. "If anything were to happen to me or—" she shrugged "—if I just disappear, this shop and the business are yours."

"What in the world?" Jodie looked from the document to Meg. "Are you going somewhere? Has something happened that I don't know about?"

"No," Meg lied. She'd grown very good at lying over the years. "I just don't have anyone to leave things to, and I wanted to be sure that if I died or if I just decided I was done with things here that you take over. I see how good you are with the animals and the customers. I feel comfortable leaving all of it with you—if something happens. I also left something for Dottie. It's all upstairs on my desk. This is more or less a letter of instruction."

Jodie shook her head, refolded the document. "This isn't right. There's something you're not telling me."

Meg took the document from her, tucked it back into the envelope and placed it in the register drawer. "You don't need to worry," she argued. "Just know that it's here. I want you to take care of this place if I'm not here. Got it?"

Jodie blinked, emotion shining in her eyes. "Well, of course I will. But this sounds like—I don't know—something permanent."

"Hey," Meg said, "it's just insurance. Smart businesswomen don't take chances."

Jodie did another of those slow nods. "Okay. I guess I understand."

Meg hugged her. "Good. Now I have stuff to do, so you carry on." She gestured to the door. "Great job getting that taken care of first thing."

Jodie smiled, her cheeks a little flushed. "Thanks. I love this shop. I hope you know that I will do my very best to run it just like you, if ever the need arises."

Meg smiled. "See. I did the right thing."

With that out of the way, Meg went upstairs and checked her studio one last time just to make sure there was nothing else she needed, then she used the back stairs to leave. A female voice she recognized as one of the shop's regular customers told her Jodie was preoccupied. Just as well, Meg wasn't so good with goodbyes. She loaded into her truck and drove away.

Her eyes burned, but she refused to cry. She had enjoyed her life here. She'd hoped it would last, but there had never been and never would be any guarantees.

Not this time or the next.

Griffin Residence
Sundown Road
11:00 a.m.

ALL MORNING GRIFF hadn't been able to shake the feeling that something bad was about to happen. That overwhelming sense of doom just lingered and lingered. Especially after Meg had left.

When he spotted Ernie's SUV rolling along his driveway, he understood his instincts had been right. Whatever news his friend was here to deliver, Griff suspected it was not good.

He waited on the porch, one shoulder propped against the post on the right of the steps. "Morning," he said as his friend climbed out of his SUV.

"Morning." Ernie glanced around. "Is Meg here?"

Griff shook his head. "She had to drop off that rescued beagle at Lonnie's, and then she was going to check in at Pampered Paws. What's up?"

"Good. I was hoping I could speak to you alone," Ernie admitted. "There's something you need to know about Meg."

"All right. Come on in."

Ernie followed him inside. "Do we need something stronger than coffee to do this?" Griff asked, bracing for what he feared was going to be the bad he'd sensed coming. He wasn't usually one to drink in the middle of the morning, but his entire being was poised on the edge of panic.

"Another time maybe," Ernie suggested.

"I'm guessing we should sit."

Ernie nodded. "Yeah. That's probably a good idea."

Griff took the few steps to the living room and dropped into his favorite chair. It was an old one, had belonged to his daddy. At some point, he needed to consider getting it recovered.

Ernie picked a spot on the sofa. "I did something I wouldn't generally do after the scene at Meg's shop yesterday."

"What's that?" However hard he tried to relax, Griff's gut just tied in bigger knots.

"Truth is," Ernie went on, "that video in the Gas and Go just kept eating at me. I couldn't get it out of my head. It…" He shook his head. "It didn't feel right."

"Meg said she'd been attacked before," Griff countered. "She took her self-defense classes very seriously. That seems pretty reasonable."

Ernie nodded slowly. "Maybe. But then when I walked into her shop and saw those two men on the floor, I realized I couldn't ignore what my gut was telling me. Something was off. This was way more than self-defense classes. This was professional."

"I can see how it looked that way," Griff admitted—he'd been a little stunned himself. "But she didn't do anything wrong. Meg is a good person, and she had every right to do what she did."

Ernie held up a hand. "I'm not trying to say she did anything wrong. I'm just… I don't know." He shrugged. "I was worried she wasn't telling me the whole story. That maybe there was something she didn't want me to know."

Griff stood and braced his hands on his hips. "Just say whatever it is you gotta say, Ernie. This conversation isn't going to get any easier."

Again, Ernie held up a hand. "Just sit down, Griff. Don't get all riled up until you hear me out."

Griff took a breath. His friend was right. He swallowed his pride and dropped back into his seat. "So, what did you do?"

"I ran her prints."

Anger pierced Griff. "Like a criminal or a suspect of some sort?"

"I felt it was my duty," Ernie argued. "And I was right to believe something was off."

Griff's anger wilted a bit. "What do you mean?"

"Meg's real name is Angela Hamilton, better known as Angel—as in the Angel of Death. The reports I got back says she's a contract killer, Griff. She worked for this ruthless drug lord out in LA. Apparently, he did something she didn't like, and she killed his son. That's why she went into hiding—which I suppose is what she's doing here—hiding. If those people find her, she's dead. Maybe anyone around her too."

For a couple of beats Griff couldn't speak. Then he snapped out of it. "That can't be right." He shook his head. He knew Meg. She was too kind and too car-

ing to be a cold-blooded killer. Even as his mind insisted that he knew this, the video from the Gas and
Go played in his head like one of those social media
reels stuck on a loop, then the images from the scene
at her shop.

"Man," Ernie said, "I'm sorry as hell to bring this to
your door, I know you like her, but this is scary stuff.
Dangerous stuff."

Griff thought of the backpack she'd carried when
she left and how she'd looked at him after that kiss
with such regret. Dread welled in his throat, and he
fought to swallow it down.

"What else did you do?" He looked at his lifelong
friend and waited to hear the rest.

"Nothing." He held up both hands as if to prove his
innocence. "I thought I'd talk to Meg, hear her side of
it before…"

"Before what?" The anger was back, like acid burning a hole inside Griff's gut.

"Before doing what I have a sworn duty to do."

Griff's mouth worked before he got the words out.
"What is it you expect me to do with this information?"

"If she comes back," Ernie said, his voice subdued
with the guilt he no doubt felt, "I need you to let me
know so I can come talk to her."

"You're going to arrest her," Griff tossed at him.
"That's your intent, isn't it?"

"No," Ernie rebutted. "I'm going to talk to her, and
we'll all figure it out from there." He stared hard at
Griff. "Meg Lewis is a good person, you're right. And

I like her too. But we have to figure this out, okay? She's a wanted criminal."

Griff nodded. "Okay."

Ernie stood. "Thanks. I realize this is hard. Just let me know when you hear from her."

Griff nodded. "Sure."

But not until he knew the whole story. No way was he throwing Meg under the bus until he was convinced there was no other choice.

No way in hell.

Chapter Eight

Monday, 11:50 a.m.

Meg had almost made it down the mountain when her cell rang.

Griff.

She couldn't answer. He would want to know when she was coming back, and she couldn't tell him that she wasn't. Not on the phone.

Or maybe the truth was she just didn't want to hear the disappointment and then the anger in his voice. She didn't want to field the questions and tell him more lies. It was better this way. *Just go.*

He and the others she had foolishly allowed herself to grow close to would be safer with her gone, where she could draw the trouble away. The less they knew, the better for all involved. Once anyone who came looking for her realized she had left town, they would follow. She'd already started the process of leaving a trail of bread crumbs to lure them after her.

She'd transferred ninety percent of the cash from her bank account to an online account based in the UK. Her readily usable assets were one of the first items that would be checked. Relocating cash was a huge tip-off that a target was on the move. She hadn't needed to move any assets to disappear; doing so was only for pointing those who came after her in the right direction she wanted them to go. Smart targets never made elementary mistakes such as that one. Those looking for her would believe she'd gotten soft or rusty, maybe both.

No matter that she'd only been in the running game for fifteen months now. She had learned from the best—from a man who'd spent his life playing the game. Those he sent to retrieve her would be looking for the sort of mistakes they expected her to make after being out of the game for more than a year.

In reality she had made only one mistake. Her cell vibrated against the seat next to her. Griff had left a voicemail.

And he was it.

Meg pulled over at the next gas station. She would fill up here using her one credit card, adding another crumb to the trail. To fill up at this gas station was a reliable indication that she was headed out of town. She climbed out, tucked her card into the slot, then made her selection and placed the nozzle into the fuel filler neck of her truck.

She watched the digits flash on the screen as the tank filled. Listening to the voicemail wasn't necessary. He probably just wanted to know if she would be back in time for lunch. Hearing his voice wouldn't benefit the necessary efforts ahead of her.

Staying wasn't an option.

Leaving was the only choice. A trail would keep her past from endangering Piney Woods, and then

she would ghost her followers like a bad boyfriend.
Nothing she hadn't done before.

Preparation was everything, and she was prepared.

The flashing digits stalled and the nozzle clicked,
indicating the tank was full. Meg removed the nozzle,
twisted on the cap and climbed back into her truck.
She tossed her cell phone onto the seat, started the
engine and reached for the gear shift.

She closed her eyes and fought a losing battle for
about five seconds, then she gave up. Snatching up her
cell, she clicked the icon for her voicemail and listened.

"Hey, Meg, I know you're probably headed back
this way by now. I just wanted to remind you to grab
some bread on your way. We used the last *two* slices
at breakfast this morning. We need bread for lunch.
See you soon."

Worry drew her face into a frown. He'd made biscuits for breakfast, not toast. The idea that his voice
had sounded a little odd and that he'd emphasized the
word *two* nudged her hard.

He was trying to tell her something.

She swore. Had someone already made it to Piney
Woods and determined her most recent location to be
at Griff's house?

Shoving the gear shift into drive, she spun out of
the gas station parking lot. Once she was on the road
headed back up the mountain, she called Jodie at the
shop.

"Pampered Paws."

"Jodie, it's Meg."

"Hey, your old friend Darlene was here looking for
you. She said the two of you went to school together."

Meg's heart stuttered to a near stop.

"I was a little hesitant to tell her anything—you know you can never be too careful these days—but she showed me a pic of you two back in high school. Loved the wild hair!"

"Wow," Meg choked out. "I haven't seen her in years." Her heart now thundered at breakneck speed. "Did she say where she's staying?"

"No but she left here headed to Griff's place to catch up with you. She couldn't believe you were living in such a small town. She said you'd always been a big-city girl."

Meg forced out a laugh. "Yeah. Darlene knows me well."

The sound of the bell over the shop's front entrance jangled.

"Oh," Jodie said. "Gotta go. Mr. Jolly is here to drop off Princess."

"'Kay. Thanks."

Meg ended the call and jammed the accelerator to the floor. She had to get to Griff. If she was lucky, it wouldn't be too late.

Sundown Road
12:10 p.m.

GRIFF DESPERATELY HOPED Meg had gotten the message he'd attempted to pass along. There were two people here looking for her. He watched the man pace back and forth at the windows framing the front of the living room. The woman, Darlene O'Neal, sat on the sofa smiling at him. She'd claimed to be an old friend of

Meg's. The man was her husband, Ted, she explained. Except Ted didn't seem the least bit friendly, much less warm toward her. He'd flashed a fake smile at Griff when he'd been introduced, and then he'd taken up watch at the front windows.

Darlene, on the other hand, had settled on the sofa and proceeded to ask Griff a thousand questions about Meg. He'd answered as vaguely as possible. He nodded and smiled now and then as Darlene waxed on about all the good times she and Meg had shared back in high school.

Griff wasn't buying any of it.

First, the jeans and plaid shirt the man—Ted—wore were obviously new. He wore his shirt unbuttoned, tail hanging out with a T-shirt beneath. The slight bulge Griff had noticed at the small of his back wasn't likely a cell phone.

The woman wore khaki colored slacks and a loose tee that sported one of Chattanooga's aquarium logos. She hadn't turned her back to him, so Griff hadn't spotted a similar bulge, but he suspected she was carrying a weapon as well. There was just something about the two that made him worry about their intentions.

"Where is your vacation taking you next?" Griff asked when the woman paused in her lengthy monologue about Meg. The man had said they were on a cross-country vacation. They'd both taken leaves of absences from their stressful jobs and were seeing the sights wherever the road took them.

Darlene smiled. Ted glanced over.

Not a question either had expected.

"Gatlinburg," she said. "We can't wait to do a little mountain hiking."

Griff hummed a note of question. "I would've thought you'd be dying to visit Nashville first. Everyone seems to love that scene."

"Already been there," Ted said. "I don't like country music."

Darlene smiled another of those big fake smiles. "We're more into the rock thing. Meg and I used to pretend we were groupies for whatever the hottest rock band was."

Funny. Meg had told him that she'd loved country music since she was a kid. It was all her parents ever listened to. It was all he'd ever heard her listen to.

Next to Griff, Raymond made a distressed sound. He, too, was aware something wasn't right. Maybe he sensed Griff's tension.

"I should let him out," Griff said, standing.

Both Ted and Darlene visibly tensed. Ted shifted to face Griff, his frame rigid. Darlene straightened from the relaxed position she'd taken on the sofa.

Griff shrugged. "He's an old dog. Probably needs to pee."

Darlene stood abruptly. "I changed my mind about the water. I'd love a glass."

"Sure." He headed toward the kitchen, patting his thigh so Raymond would follow. He didn't have to glance back to know Darlene brought up the rear. She had no intention of allowing him out of her sight.

In the kitchen, Griff opened the back door. "Go on, buddy."

Raymond stared up at him as if to ask if he were sure.

Griff hitched his head toward the yard. "Go on. Do your business."

Reluctantly, Raymond moseyed on out. Griff closed the door behind him and turned back to his guest. "Ice or no?"

"Just water," she said.

He rounded up a clean glass and ran it two-thirds full of tap water. "Here you go." He passed the glass to her.

"Thanks." She took a sip and made an appreciative sound. "We don't have water right out of the tap like this back home."

Griff wasn't sure what he was supposed to say to that. "Big cities come with their own issues, I guess."

"They do," she agreed.

He said nothing else. She said nothing else. After about a minute, she sat her glass on the counter and looked expectantly at him, so he headed back to the living room. She followed.

"She should be here by now," Ted said, seemingly to himself.

"I'm sure she'll be here any minute. She had to stop for bread," Darlene reminded him as she settled back on the sofa. "Be careful that she doesn't see you," she warned her supposed husband. "We don't want to ruin the surprise."

Ted had already moved their car to the back of the house. Griff hadn't bought the surprise thing either. He was no lawman or detective, but he knew an ambush when he saw one.

Frankly, his head was still reeling at the information Ernie had passed along. He wasn't entirely sure he bought the story. Not that Ernie would lie. For that matter, he'd shown Griff the records or so-called rap sheet he'd printed out. Meg's prints had matched this Angela "Angel" Hamilton's. Didn't matter. He knew Meg and she wouldn't...

Kill anyone...

But she had. She had killed Zyair Jones during the Gas and Go robbery. She could easily have killed the two that broke into her shop.

Griff swallowed back the bitter taste of dread and regret. He couldn't have been that wrong about her. He'd always considered himself a fairly decent judge of character. Surely he hadn't been that far off the mark with Meg.

Ernie had been flabbergasted as well. He kept saying none of it made sense. Although he'd suspected something was off, he hadn't anticipated it would be something straight out of a spy movie. Griff studied the two people seated in his living room who waited for Meg to arrive. But these two, they gave off exactly the kind of vibe he would expect from a hired assassin. Had these two obvious imposters come here to assassinate Meg?

His gut twisted, and the ability to draw in a breath grew more difficult. He had to do something. He couldn't just sit here and allow Meg to walk into a trap. He'd done the only thing he could on the phone when the two had urged him to make sure Meg was headed back. Honestly, he hadn't expected her to come back after what Ernie had told him. And maybe she wouldn't have if he hadn't called her and left that odd voicemail. If that was the case, then whatever these two had planned was on him.

His cell vibrated. He reached into his back pocket. Again, the two visitors came to a new level of attention. That wasn't suspicious at all. Ignoring their reaction, he pulled out his cell.

Meg.

He answered the call. "Hey."

"Hey," she said. "I'm almost there, but I had a flat tire just as I turned into your driveway. I can walk to the house, but I just wanted to let you know why it was taking so long."

"I can drive out there and help you fix the tire," he suggested.

Darlene leaned forward. Her eyes narrowed.

Ted surveyed the yard, then glanced at Griff before returning his attention to the window.

"That would probably be better," Meg said. "I'll just wait here then."

"Be right there." Griff ended the call as he stood.

"Has something happened?" Darlene asked, rising to her feet as well.

"No big deal." Griff slid his cell into his back pocket. "She has a flat on her truck, but she's just down the driveway at the road. It'll take ten minutes maybe to change the tire."

"I'll help." Ted stepped away from the window.

Griff made a face. "You don't need to do that. If you've ever changed a tire, you know it's a one-person job. You two can wait here and—"

"We'll go with you," Darlene insisted. "We can take the surprise to her."

"All righty then." Griff looked from one to the other. "I can get my keys or we can walk. It's only about three quarters of a mile."

"We should take your truck," Ted suggested.

Griff went to the kitchen and snagged his keys from the rack by the back door. When he turned to go back to the living room, he wasn't surprised to find Darlene watching him from the doorway.

"I simply can't wait to see the look on her face," she said, feigning excitement.

Or maybe she was excited by what she had planned for Meg. Griff felt sick at the idea.

"I'm sure she'll be happy to see you." It was the best he could come up with, given what he expected was about to go down.

Raymond had stretched out on the porch along with the other dogs.

"You have a lot of pets," Darlene noted.

"I rescue pets," Griff explained. "These are all animals that have been abandoned."

Ted grunted as he scanned the dogs. "I never understood why someone would abandon a dog when it's far easier just to put them out of their misery."

If Griff hadn't already disliked the guy, he damned sure did now. "Some people shouldn't have pets."

Another grunt was the guy's only response.

Griff climbed behind the wheel. Ted opened the passenger side door and waited for Darlene. It was a flat-out miracle in Griff's opinion that the guy had any sort of manners.

"Maybe I'll just walk," Darlene said. "It's a nice

day. You two go on and get a head start on changing that tire."

Griff didn't like the idea, but there was little he could do about it. Instead, he started the truck and backed toward the barn, then headed to the road. He drove slower than usual and kept an eye on the woman strolling along the gravel road behind him.

"You don't need to drive so slow because of her," Ted mentioned. "She'll catch up."

"I'm driving slow," Griff said, resisting the urge to clench his teeth, "to prevent leaving a cloud of dust for her to walk through."

He could drive faster without that concern; the road was mostly gravel after all. But he was banking on this guy not knowing the difference.

Ted didn't argue the point.

A couple of the longest minutes he'd ever experienced later, Meg's truck came into view. Sure enough, the left front tire was flat. He parked. Scanned the area for Meg. Didn't see her, but the jack laid on the ground next to the spare tire. A part of Griff hoped this was some aspect of her plan to evade this bizarre couple. But maybe it was just all the movies he'd seen that put the notion in his head.

Griff parked and got out. Ted did the same. Darlene hadn't rounded the curve in the long driveway just yet.

When Meg didn't appear, Griff called her name. "Meg?" He walked over to the truck, surveyed the deflated tire. He frowned. Looked as if the sidewall had been punctured.

"Where is she?" Ted scanned the surrounding woods.

"Meg?" Griff called again. "She has to be here—"

The blast of a gunshot silenced him. He shifted to see Ted preparing to fire a second time.

Griff started toward the other man. "What the hell?"

A second shot exploded in the air.

Ted stood for a moment, looking startled. The weapon he'd been holding slipped from his hand and clattered on the gravel. Griff blinked, stared at the hole in the man's forehead.

Ted dropped to the ground.

"Run!"

Griff shifted his stunned gaze toward the trees.

"Run, damn it!"

Meg.

He couldn't see her, but the voice was definitely hers.

Darlene appeared in the distance.

She was running now.

Gun.

Her arms were extended and she was holding a gun.

Griff lunged for the tree line.

Another gunshot sounded.

The bullet nicked a tree to his right.

Griff darted behind another larger tree. He held completely still. Listened.

Another gunshot.

A scream.

"Oh God." He peeked past the trunk that concealed him. If Meg was hit…

He eased from his hiding place and moved carefully toward the road in the direction of the scream.

Darlene sat on the ground. Meg stood over her, the weapon in her hand pointed at the downed woman.

"Get up!" Meg ordered as she tucked something—another gun—into the waistband of her jeans at the small of her back.

The images that had filled Griff's head when Ernie told him he suspected Meg was this Angel, this assassin, flooded his brain now.

Before he realized he'd stepped from the tree line, he was moving toward her.

"Get. Up."

Meg stepped back as the other woman struggled to rise. Blood had spread from her right shoulder toward her chest. She cradled her right arm which hung against her side.

"Don't come any closer, Griff."

He stalled. Needed a moment to find his voice. "What the hell is going on, Meg? Who are these people?"

"Who sent you?" Meg demanded of the woman who'd called herself Darlene.

Darlene, or whoever the hell she was, grinned. "Who do you think sent me?"

Meg aimed her weapon at Darlene's face. "Answer the question."

"Your old friend. He wasn't happy to find out you were still alive, so he sent us to rectify the situation." She turned up her left hand. "You understand. He can't have you continuing to breathe under the circumstances."

"That's too bad for you," Meg said.

Griff moved a step closer. "What're you going to do?"

Meg suddenly reached back with her left hand and

whipped the weapon from her waistband and pointed it at Griff. "I said don't come any closer."

He froze. Something like fire rushed through him—a weird combination of anger and disappointment.

Darlene laughed. "You going to shoot him too? I'm guessing your Goody Two-shoes friend here has no clue who you are." She looked past Meg and directly at Griff. "You don't know a killer when you meet one?"

"Shut up," Meg growled as she lowered the weapon she had aimed at Griff. "Turn around," she said to Darlene.

The burn of anger roared hotter through Griff, overriding the other emotions. He might not have seen past whatever facade Meg had built, but he wasn't a fool. She was not a bad person, no matter what his eyes were telling him right now.

Was that his heart talking or his brain? If it was the former, he could be in trouble here.

Darlene reluctantly turned around. Meg shoved the extra weapon back into her waistband and approached the other woman. She checked her waistband, ran a hand down and then up her legs from the tops of her shoes to her pockets. Then she checked her pockets. She removed something.

Griff peered harder to try and see what Meg had taken from the woman's pocket, but he couldn't make it out.

Meg glanced back at him. "I need your help."

Her words hit him square in the chest. "What?"

She hitched her head for him to come there. "I need your help," she repeated.

He made his way to where the two stood, stepping over a fallen tree.

Meg handed the object toward him. "When I get her to my truck, use this to secure her left hand to the steering wheel."

Zip tie. The object was a nylon zip tie. He took it from her and nodded.

"Start walking." Meg nudged Darlene.

They walked through the woods back to the two trucks abandoned on his driveway. His gut clenched at the sight of Ted whatever-his-name-was still lying face up on the ground, a hole in his forehead.

"You killed him."

His own words startled him as if his brain hadn't realized his mouth was speaking.

"I did."

He met her gaze. "Why?"

"Because he would have killed you if I hadn't."

"Don't believe her," Darlene shouted. "Ted and I are cops from Los Angeles. We're here to take her back. She's wanted for murder."

Griff blinked once, twice.

"If you believe that," Meg said, urging the other woman toward her truck, "I have some oceanfront property in Arizona to sell you."

Griff nodded. He knew Darlene was lying. If she and Ted had been cops they would have said so up front and showed some ID.

When they reached Meg's truck, she opened the driver side door and nudged the woman in the ribs with the muzzle of her gun. "Get in."

Darlene did as she was told, though her glare was lethal. It was clear she wanted to tear Meg's head off.

Meg glanced at Griff then. "Secure her."

While Meg held the gun aimed at Darlene's head, he secured her left wrist to the steering wheel. The keys weren't in the ignition, and the tire was flat, making an escape unlikely unless she chewed off the zip tie. It didn't appear she could move her right arm. The bleeding was worse.

Griff stepped back. "She needs medical attention."

Meg stared at the other woman. "But she doesn't deserve it."

Griff started to argue with her, but she faced him. "Let's go. You drive."

Griff glanced at Darlene one last time before doing as Meg said.

"You just going to leave me to die?" Darlene shouted after them.

When he and Meg had climbed into his truck, he noticed she had at some point grabbed her backpack, and more importantly, she still had the gun, and it was aimed at him.

"You going to shoot me too?"

"Just drive. Toward Chattanooga."

He started the truck.

"I need your phone."

He gave her his cell, fastened his seat belt and then shifted into Drive.

When he was on the road heading away from his place, she took her eyes off him long enough to do something on his phone.

Several thoughts zoomed through his mind. He

could wreck the truck, and that would stop whatever this was. He could just stop and demand answers.

She tossed his phone onto the middle of the bench seat between them, then fastened her seat belt.

He glanced at her again as he drove.

"I sent a text to Ernie," she said. "Told him there were two thugs from LA in your driveway, one dead, one injured. He should call for backup because the woman is incredibly dangerous and an ambulance because she's injured. So don't look at me that way."

Before he could say anything, his phone started to vibrate. He glanced at it, saw Ernie's name on the screen. "You should let me talk to him."

Meg grabbed the phone, accepted the call and set it to speaker. Ernie's voice shouted, "What the hell is going on, Griff?"

"This is Meg," she said in answer. "Listen to me, Ernie. Don't be fooled by the injured woman. She is very dangerous. She will kill you if she gets a chance. Keep your weapon trained on her until the paramedics arrive, and then do the same while they attend to her. She will kill whoever she has to in order to escape."

"Meg, where is Griff and what the hell is happening?"

"I'm here," Griff said. "I'm okay. I don't know exactly what's going on…" He glanced at Meg. "But what she said is true."

"Remember what I said, Ernie," she reiterated, then she ended the call and threw the phone out the window.

"What the hell?" Griff demanded, dividing his attention between her and the road.

"Take the next left," she said. "We don't want to meet Ernie on his way to your place."

Griff gritted his teeth and tightened his grip on the steering wheel. "Where are we going?"

"As soon as I figure that out," Meg said, "I'll let you know."

Griff wanted to believe those people back there were the bad guys—just like she said. And that she was actually not this Angela Hamilton.

But the fact that she kept her weapon aimed in his general direction warned him there was a good chance he was wrong.

Chapter Nine

1:30 p.m.

How had this happened so fast?

Meg had known time was short after that reporter managed a shot of her. But that had only been last night. Even as it was picked up on the AP, Lorenzo's people couldn't have seen it and gotten here this fast. It wasn't possible. There had to be another explanation.

Damn it. She'd wanted to lead the bastards away from here, not bring them in like long-lost cousins.

"Is it true?"

The sound of Griff's voice snapped Meg from her musings. "Is what true?" She shook herself and realized she was still holding the weapon at the ready. She lifted the top of the console and placed it inside. She had to shake this haze of disbelief. She had to be better prepared. On her toes. His life—she looked at him—depended on her.

Griff glanced at the console, then at her. "Is your name really Angela Hamilton?"

Anger stoked in her belly. "Did she tell you that?"

Lizbeth Franks, aka Darlene, whatever she'd called herself today, was one of Lorenzo's top guns. Being female and on the petite side worked to her benefit. Opponents always underestimated her physical ability and her intellectual ruthlessness. The woman was utterly heartless. She would shoot her own mother if it served her purpose.

"You mean the woman you shot?"

So, it was that way, was it? "At least she was still breathing," Meg allowed, "unlike her friend."

Griff looked at her again, and this time his gaze lingered long enough for her to wonder if he'd forgotten he was driving.

"You killed that man."

"We discussed that already," she pointed out. "If I hadn't, you would be dead now. Me too, assuming he could catch me."

She understood that Griff did not fully comprehend any of this. Who would? How many people experienced this kind of situation in their lifetimes? Sure, there were criminals out there who shot each other up on the street. Thugs who robbed places like the Gas and Go all the time. But this was a whole different level. That part he obviously got. *This* was something only those who lived in the world she had once lived in fully grasped. It was glamorized, badly, in movies and in novels. But this was not a movie or a novel. This was real life, and fearlessness along with finesse would be required to survive.

Griff braked for a traffic light that had turned red. He turned to her. "Who are you?"

Meg considered this for a moment before she answered. Part of her desperately wanted to tell him everything. To make him understand her situation so he wouldn't look at her that way. But that would put him in more danger than he'd already fallen into. The truth was too dangerous. Just being close to it had already put his life in jeopardy.

Still, she needed to give him something. As much for herself as for him, she didn't want him to feel about her the way she suspected he did right now. She couldn't bear the way he looked at her.

"You can call me Elle." Her father had called her Elle. She'd been named after her grandmother Eleanor.

"So, you're not Angela Hamilton, aka Angel, a cold-blooded assassin?"

"I recognize that it may seem like I am when you consider what's happened the past couple of days. But I have never taken a life unless mine or someone else's was at stake and there was no other option except to intervene with deadly force. If I was a merciless killer, those two men who invaded my shop would be dead. Lizbeth—Darlene—would definitely be done. She doesn't deserve to keep breathing, but I chose not to make that decision since I had the situation under control without having to end her life."

Griff pressed her with those golden eyes that made her want to say whatever was necessary to reverse this situation.

"Then why are your fingerprints connected to that name?"

Her jaw dropped. "How do you know that?" She had figured Darlene or her dead friend gave him that name.

A horn blew behind them.

Meg put her hand on the console as she whipped her head around. The driver behind them threw up his hands in question. Meg realized the light had changed back to green, and they'd just been sitting there. Griff realized the same and hit the accelerator.

"Ernie worried there was something else going on after the attack on you by the Joneses, so he ran your prints. The Los Angeles Police Department responded almost immediately."

Of course they had. Great. No wonder Lorenzo had gotten someone here so quickly. He had eyes and ears in the LAPD. Same with the sheriff's department in Los Angeles County and numerous others. The man owned the West Coast.

When Lorenzo didn't hear from Lizbeth in a timely manner, or if he did, assuming Ernie allowed her a phone call, he would send others. He wouldn't stop until she was dead.

She had to get out of here.

"Where are we going?"

She needed to think. Things were complicated now. There would be no slipping away with no strings, leaving this man and all else behind. Lizbeth would believe that Griff was in this with Meg. She would hunt him down and use him for luring Meg back.

"We need to hide for a bit." She considered the options. "I need to figure out my next move."

Silence radiated between them for a mile or so. Meg wished it hadn't come to this. She wished Griff had never needed to know about her past. If she hadn't seen the guy at the Gas and Go—but then Jennifer would likely be dead—maybe she would still have her carefully structured quiet life.

But her life was not more important than Jennifer's.

Meg had done the right thing, and she would do it again. *Damn it.*

"I might know a place."

Meg waited for him to go on.

"Ernie has a cabin."

She laughed. "I'm not sure that's a good idea, considering he thinks I'm some sort of hired killer, and this woman who called herself Darlene will spin an even nastier tale—assuming she doesn't kill him."

"Ernie won't do anything if I tell him we need time."

Meg wondered if he really believed Ernie would go along with the idea. "Ernie is a lawman," she reminded him. "I'm not so sure he's going to want to go along with this idea, even for a lifelong best friend."

Griff sent her a look. "He's worried about you. About us. He will give you a chance."

Meg contemplated his statement for a moment before saying more. "Does that mean you're giving me a chance as well?"

She might be getting soft, but she wasn't a fool. This could be a ruse to get her captured and him free of her. If she were in his shoes, that was exactly what she would do.

"Why wouldn't I?"

That was the big question. Why wouldn't he? Because he was a good person.

No question. She knew this with complete certainty. Ernie was a good person too.

"Okay. We'll go to Ernie's cabin and regroup."

It might be the last decision she ever made, but she was willing to take the risk.

Deep Woods Trail
3:20 p.m.

ERNIE'S CABIN WAS, as the road leading to it suggested, deep in the woods. Perched on a creek bank and miles away from Piney Woods. Miles away from basically anything actually. As long as Ernie stuck by his word, Meg could live with the situation for long enough to pull together a workable plan.

They'd stopped at a convenience store and grabbed a few things well ahead of arriving in this area, paying cash. A quick call from the store's landline to Ernie took care of a few loose ends and garnered a bit of an update. But she made sure Griff gave his friend the least amount of information necessary. Not that Meg expected Lorenzo to have access to someone inside the Hamilton County Sheriff's Department, but she couldn't be sure of anything. The man had money and power, and he was the epitome of ruthless. He wanted Meg nearly as much as he wanted his next breath. She doubted the scumbag had ever wanted anyone dead as badly as he wanted her that way.

The cabin's front door opened, and Meg jumped in spite of knowing that it was only Griff.

"I parked the truck behind the cabin."

So far, Griff hadn't asked any additional questions and he'd cooperated without hesitation. She imagined that would change as soon as the initial shock and denial had worn off. There was a lot she wanted to tell him, but she still wasn't sure it was the right thing to do.

And even if it was safe to do so, how did you walk

back more than a year and multiple layers of subter-
fuge? She had lied to him repeatedly. Nothing about
the tale she'd spun had been true. Well, except for
growing up in Bakersfield on a farm and her love of
animals. All of that had been the truth.

"Thanks." For however long it lasted, she genuinely
appreciated his help.

They should eat. That would buy her some time
before he thought of more questions and would hopefully calm her jangling nerves. Bologna sandwiches
had never been among her favorites, but the selec-
tions at the convenience store hadn't been that great.
She could eat a dead rat if it was roasted just right—
if the need arose. She'd only had to do that once. She
doubted sharing the experience would help her build
her case about not being a ruthless assassin.

Since Griff leaned against the counter saying nothing, she opted to take the initiative. She removed the
bologna from the fridge, where she'd stored it only
moments ago. Next, she grabbed the mayo and mus-
tard and bread. A couple of soft drinks and chips.

He watched as she prepared the plates. The cabin's
kitchen area, which was actually a corner in the main
room, was well stocked as far as dishes and utensils, pans and dry and canned goods were concerned.
There was electricity and running water, including
hot water. So, not so rustic as far as the necessities
were concerned. A bathroom with a shower. But only
one bed that stood in another corner of the big room.

This should be an interesting night. The way she
saw it, her biggest problem would be not allowing

her desperation to guide her. Desperation never led to anything good.

Her gaze landed on the man who complicated an already complex situation even more. In more ways than he could fathom.

"We should eat," she suggested as she pulled out a chair.

He moved away from the counter and took the seat across from her. They ate. No talking. Just eating, drinking and glancing at each other and then away. It was somehow disturbing and yet oddly sensual.

When he'd eaten every morsel on his plate, he pushed it away and stared directly into her eyes. "Who are you?"

She downed the last of her drink. Made a decision. "I can't tell you all you want to know because that information could be a problem for you later. I don't want to create more problems for you."

"I've got Lonnie taking care of my animals and Ernie keeping watch for any new arrivals in town," Griff said.

Ernie had agreed to covertly inform Jodie to close up shop and lay low for a few days.

With that one call she and Griff had done things they hadn't wanted to do. The difference was that this was her problem, not his. The steps he had taken were out of the goodness of his heart, not necessity.

She owed him for giving her the benefit of the doubt.

"You owe me the truth."

He'd read her mind. "You're right." She stood, stacked their plates and headed to the sink. She washed the plates and the utensils she'd used to make the sandwiches, then dried her hands and turned to face him.

He waited, still seated at the table, watching her every move.

"My name, like I already told you, is Eleanor, Elle. I'm from Bakersfield, California. Both my parents are dead, just like I told you before. I have no siblings. No ex-husbands or serious relationships. All the things I told you about my personal life were true. I grew up on a farm, etcetera."

"You lied about everything else," he countered. The distrust and disappointment in his voice and expression was a punch to the gut.

"Only about my career. Everything else was all true."

"Is your former career the reason these people came after you?"

She nodded. "The man they work for is very powerful. If you believe in heaven and hell, good and evil, then he's the devil. The one you heard stories about as a kid."

"What does that mean exactly? The devil?" Griff's voice warned that she'd lost ground with the analogy.

Okay, back it up. She took a breath. "It means I took something that belonged to him, and he's spent nearly a year and a half trying to find me so he can have his revenge. Now, because of Ernie running my prints, he knows where I am."

A scowl claimed his face. "You stole something from him?"

"In a manner of speaking." She wasn't prepared to explain. She'd already told him too much.

"You want me to go along with whatever this is, but you won't tell me the whole truth."

She braced her hands on the counter on either side of her. "I'll be out of here by morning. I just need you to give me until then."

He stood, turned his back on her and walked to the door. "I need some air."

She hated like hell to say this, but she had to. "Leave the keys to your truck."

He glared at her for a moment before tossing the key fob on the sofa, then he walked out the door.

That move hadn't gained her any ground either.

Nothing she could do about that. Maybe he would understand later.

Doubtful. She closed her eyes and pressed her fingertips there. How the hell was she going to keep him safe from what was coming? If she took off, Lorenzo's people would just find him and torture him to death in hopes of getting information on her.

Really, how could she possibly save him now without taking him with her?

He had family. A mother. A sister. Friends. A life. He wasn't going willingly. She was a fool to even consider he might.

But if she left him here…

She knew what would happen. There was no question.

He would die, and his death would be her fault.

GRIFF WALKED TO the end of the narrow drive that twisted through the trees along the creek bank. He and Ernie had come here as kids. Had poker nights here once a month to this day. It was quiet, way off the beaten path and very few people knew about it. It was their getaway. Their man cave. Only now it felt like a prison, like hell on earth. Griff wanted to do the right thing. He wanted to help Meg.

But what if trusting her was wrong?

Ernie wasn't so sure about Griff bringing Meg— or whatever her name was—here, but he'd deferred to Griff's judgment. So far, no one else had shown up asking for Meg. At least not as far as Ernie knew at this point. The woman, Darlene—Lizbeth, Meg had called her—wasn't talking. Ernie hadn't given her a phone call yet. He intended to put it off as long as the law allowed. All because Griff had asked him to trust him.

But what if trusting Meg and, by extension, him was a mistake? What if he got Ernie killed?

His gut twisted hard.

If Griff still had his phone, he'd call and ask Ernie what the chances were that the criminal record he'd pulled up on Meg was somehow faked. She insisted that wasn't her name and that she wasn't a hired killer.

Griff had to admit he believed her, but what if his emotions had clouded his judgment? He had feelings for her, feelings not so easily dismissed.

Damn it.

She said she needed until morning and then she would be gone. Could he let her go like that? Pretend she never existed? Go on with his life like he hadn't met her?

He thought of the way she took care of the animals, of how she took care of the people around her. What he knew about her just didn't fit with what he'd witnessed the past couple of days. It sure as hell didn't fit with what Ernie had found.

Griff paused and recounted the facts.

She had dropped that guy—Ted—from a serious distance with a handgun. She was no amateur when it came to firearms. Then there was the way she'd handled herself. Having him secure the woman to that steering wheel. The way she'd taken down the guy in the Gas and Go. Then, she'd taken down the two in her shop without a weapon.

No question her actions could fit with a hired-gun type. On the contrary, she could just as easily fit the description of a well-trained cop. He toyed with the idea for a moment. Made sense. Fit with her caring personality more so than the idea of an assassin.

If she had been a cop, why not just tell him? Why all the lies and the running?

Maybe she'd been a witness to a crime. It was possible that was why she was on the run. But that scenario wouldn't explain her special skill set. Or why she wasn't in some sort of witness protection program.

Griff ran a hand through his hair, turned and stared at the cabin. If she had been a cop, why wasn't she willing to tell him?

He walked slowly back to the cabin. Maybe if he gave her a little more time, she would decide it was safe to tell him more. He recognized that on some level, she didn't trust him enough to tell him the truth. Or maybe it was like she said—too dangerous to tell him.

He'd thought they were friends. Had hoped they

would become more than friends. That kiss they had shared sure seemed to suggest there was more.

Moving with more determination now, he approached the cabin. She had come out onto the porch and settled into one of the rocking chairs. Same ones that had been here for more than three decades.

"I've been thinking." He climbed onto the porch and settled into the other rocking chair. "Where did you learn to shoot the way you do? I mean, there's good and then there's really good. You are really good. Most folks on farms learn to shoot rifles. You took Ted out from a hell of a distance with a handgun."

"Lots of training." She sighed. "I was the best in my class."

He'd like to believe he was so charming she hadn't even realized he'd been questioning her, but he knew better.

"Same class as the self-defense one?"

"In a manner of speaking."

She wasn't going to make this easy.

Time to ad-lib. "Ernie says the training for a cop is intense like that. Focus on marksmanship skills and self-defense."

She said nothing.

"So, this guy—the devil, you called him—he was a bad guy. You were working on an investigation involving him. You took something from him in an effort to bring him down, but something went wrong and you ended up burned."

She smiled. "That's a hell of a story, Griff. You might want to pitch it to a movie producer."

Frustration lit across his senses. "You could at least tell me if I'm getting warm."

She watched him for a long time before she responded. He had decided she wasn't going to when she finally spoke. "You're a good guy, Griff. I truly regret being the reason you've been dragged into this. I had a plan. Sadly, it just didn't work out."

"Because Ernie ran your prints." He got it now. "His doing so tipped off someone who informed this super bad guy, and he sent his people after you."

"Something like that."

He was getting closer. "If this Darlene character gets a chance to call him, he'll know he needs to send someone else."

"Unfortunately. Even without a call, he will be suspicious by tomorrow. He has no patience for lingering. He expects results on the immediate side."

"Does he want you brought to him, or does he just want you dead?"

"Based on Lizbeth's appearance, I'm guessing the latter. She isn't known for her finesse with targets. She's much better at terminating than transporting."

Griff had come to that same conclusion as well. "Is there anything I can do to help?"

She leaned forward, pressed her forearms to her knees and clasped her hands. She stared at her hands for a moment before meeting his gaze. "I'm afraid there isn't anything anyone can do. I'll either outmaneuver him or I won't."

The barrage of emotions that churned inside Griff were impossible to isolate. The anger and frustration and worry and regret coalesced into something resembling dread and fear, but far more potent.

"I want you to know that whatever you've done, my opinion of you has not changed." He fixed his gaze on hers. "I believe in you, Meg—Elle. I will do whatever I can to help you through this."

She smiled. "You're a really nice guy, Griff. You deserve a good life and a romantic partner who can give you as much as you give everyone in your path. But there is nothing you can do to help me. There's nothing anyone can do."

She'd said those same words before, but he had decided that was one part of her story he wasn't going to believe.

She wasn't the only one who could develop a plan.

Chapter Ten

Deep Woods Trail
9:00 p.m.

It was dark.

Time to move.

Meg—she'd focused so hard on calling herself Meg for the past fifteen months that she couldn't even think of herself as Elle now that she'd been outed—had made a decision on her next step. For the plan to work, she had to find a way to keep Griff out of sight for a while.

She glanced at him. He'd insisted on heating up a can of soup and then that they both ate said soup. The crackers he'd found were a little stale but not so bad. She wasn't complaining. The ability to perform critical thinking and to physically outmaneuver the enemy required two things: sleep and sustenance.

The one thing she understood with absolute certainty after spending the past few hours shut up in this small cabin with him was that he was determined to help her survive this situation. This was exactly why she should never have allowed herself to get so close to the folks in Piney Woods. People like Jodie and Dottie, and certainly Griff, cared about her and wanted to help with whatever she needed.

But they didn't adequately comprehend the situation. This was not about picking up an extra shift or taking home a few dogs to foster. This was about facing people who killed for a living. People who enjoyed killing. People with no conscience. Unfortunately, there was no simple solution to her dilemma.

The one thing she needed right now was to be alone—to be abandoned by those who cared about her. It was the only way to ensure their protection, and even then she worried that might not be enough.

But if she got away clean and Griff laid low for a few days while she laid out a new trail for her pursuers to follow, he might just survive the coming storm.

She glanced at his back as he put away the bowls they had used and he'd washed and dried. She should have helped, but she'd been staring out the window in deep thought and hadn't known what he was doing until he was done. Since it was dark, it was time to put her plan into action.

"Do you think Ernie has any flashlights around here?" She strolled toward the kitchen area. "If the generator runs out of fuel, we'll need flashlights."

He glanced around. "I'm sure there are some around here somewhere."

"Mind if I poke around?"

"Be my guest." He tossed the towel onto the counter. "I'll help."

Meg started with the side tables in the living room area. She found poker cards and game chips. A lighter. Pens, pads of paper. Scissors. A couple of cans of beer. She laughed, held up a can. "Someone was hiding his stash."

Griff grinned. "That would be Joey Hurt. He used to be a deputy here. He joined us a couple of times. That was his favorite brand. No one else liked it, so he always brought his own supply."

Meg placed the beer back in the drawer. She stood, stretched then moved on to the bedside table. She dropped to her knees and pulled open the first drawer. Right on top was a pair of binoculars. "These could be handy." She placed them on the table.

"We like watching the deer come to the creek for water."

"Birds too?" She glanced at him. She imagined there were lots of bird species and wildlife.

"Sometimes." He shrugged. "Mostly the four-legged animals."

"Aha." Meg lifted a pair of metal handcuffs from the drawer. "Did you use these in your poker games?"

Griff laughed as he closed the last of the cabinet doors. "I can't answer that question. You'll have to ask Ernie. He's the only one who ever comes here with a romantic interest."

"A romantic interest." She nodded. "Did you ever bring a romantic interest here?" None of her business, but she couldn't help herself.

"Not me." Griff opened a drawer next to the sink. "I prefer…" He stopped talking as if he'd realized he was about to say something too personal.

She shrugged and placed the handcuffs on the table. These could definitely come in handy. The fact that he hadn't used them on someone like Rhianna the casserole queen was all the better. Funny how she had absolutely no right to feel anything remotely resembling jealousy, and still she did. Just one more indication of how far over the line she had allowed herself to go. Doing a mental eye roll, she shifted her attention back to going through the drawers.

"I've been thinking." Griff walked over and sat down on the edge of the bed.

She erased the immediate reaction from her face. The last thing she needed was for him to pick up on any impatience or regret at the idea that he wanted to help. She needed him to believe his help and advice were welcome. She also didn't want him picking up on her possessiveness toward him.

"About?" she asked innocently.

"About the situation." He let his impatience show a little.

"Okay. Tell me your thoughts." She sat back on her heels, gave him her undivided attention and waited for him to go on.

"Ernie can go to Sheriff Norwood. She's good. She might be able to help."

Why couldn't Meg make him see that the more people drawn into this, the higher the body count would rise? Ernie, the sheriff—no one could fix this. No matter how good, no matter how well intentioned. This was not that simple. "I wish she could, but that isn't likely. I appreciate the suggestion though."

"Sit with me." He patted the mattress beside him. "You've been pacing the floor and staring out that window for hours. Now you're prowling around in drawers. You need a break. I know you're worried, but you keep blowing off my suggestions."

Meg moved up to the bed. "Really, I appreciate your suggestions. I appreciate your friendship. I just don't want anyone else to get hurt by this, and that's what will happen if other people get involved. I keep telling you this, but you're not listening."

"The sheriff's department is already involved," he reminded her.

Not that she needed a reminder. "I wish that wasn't the case."

"Don't you think it would be helpful if they understood what was happening? Isn't being in the dark more dangerous to folks like Ernie?"

It was, and that was exactly why she had to get out of here as quickly as possible. She'd stayed too long after the first strike as it was.

"You're right." She made a final decision. "Maybe I should meet with them first thing in the morning to make sure they understand the situation."

The relief on his face was palpable. More guilt heaped on her shoulders. She hated lying to him.

"Great. You can call him first thing, and we'll make that happen."

"Speaking of which," she stood, "I should charge my phone."

Anything was better than staring into his hopeful eyes. She dug her charger out of her backpack and found an outlet. It wouldn't take long, so she didn't have to wait on moving forward with her plan. The sooner she was out of Griff's life, the sooner his was back on track. Distance was crucial right now. She would get out of Tennessee and let Lorenzo know she was headed his way. That should shift focus quickly enough from Piney Woods. This was the only way.

Maybe she'd head northeast and disappear into New York City. Lorenzo had contacts there as well. The bastard had contacts in every city of importance in the country. A little place like Piney Woods had felt relatively safe in the grand scheme of things. If Ernie hadn't run her prints, maybe—just maybe—she would still be safely ensconced in her made-up life.

Moments with Griff flickered through her mind like last week's recap of her favorite series. Jodie's laughter and Dottie's mothering. The best meat loaf she'd ever eaten at the diner. Raymond. God, she loved that dog. The idea of never seeing him again...

She really had to get out of here before she lost the ability to stay focused.

The longer she waited, the harder it would be to walk away.

As if he sensed her emotional struggle, Griff joined her at the window. He pulled down the worn shade. "You should relax. We'll take this to the sheriff in the morning and go from there. There's nothing else you can do tonight. Worrying won't help."

Meg braced herself. "You're right." She turned to him, looked deep into his eyes. "I think I need something to take my mind off the fact that I might never be safe, no matter where I go."

The words were for him—to garner a response— but sadly they were all too true.

He cupped her face in his hands. "I can do that," he whispered as his mouth lowered toward hers.

Her heart surged, her body trembled as his lips brushed across hers. He kissed her softly then, carefully, as if he worried she might shatter. Her hands found their way to his chest, flattened there, molding to the strength she felt beneath his shirt. His body was solid from long days of hard work. His muscles flexed beneath the pressure of her touch. She wanted so badly to unbutton his shirt, to feel the heat of his skin against her palms.

He pushed his fingers into her hair and deepened the kiss. Meg's body caught fire, reacted so intensely she barely remained standing. Her fingers were unfastening the buttons of his shirt before her brain realized what she was doing.

She just wanted to touch him, to feel him.

Catching her breath no longer mattered, slowing down was not happening. Her fingers fumbled, couldn't move fast enough. She tugged open the final button and pushed the shirt off his shoulders, and then her hands slid over his bare skin. Every nerve in her body reacted.

His fingers tangled in the hem of her tee, pulling it up and over her head. She should slow this down, but she couldn't. She wanted to feel all of him, wanted to taste him. To have him taste her, to touch her all over. They moved toward the bed. Whether he took the first step or she did, Meg couldn't be sure. Didn't matter. All that mattered was that they shed the rest of their clothes as quickly as possible.

She unfastened his jeans.

He stopped kissing her, drew back just enough to look into her eyes. "We really doing this?"

He was right. What had she been thinking? Reality slammed into her like a bucket of icy cold water splashing over her body.

You need him disabled.

Meg blinked. "Yes." She kissed him hard on the mouth until his resistance melted away. Her fingers went to his zipper again, and she slowly lowered it. He reached around her, unfastened her bra. She gasped. He dragged it down her arms and tossed it aside. Then his hands closed over her breasts. Her body seized with pleasure.

She moved his jeans down his hips, purposely leaving his boxers in place—as difficult as that task was. She so wanted to feel that part of him too. She lowered to her knees, and his eyes closed as if he couldn't bear to watch. Tugging his jeans down, he lifted first one foot and then the other so that she could pull them free.

When she stood once more, she ushered him down onto the bed. She straddled his waist, immensely grateful she still wore her jeans. She slid her palms over his chest, leaned down and caught his lower lip between her teeth.

He massaged her breasts, tugged one toward his mouth. She cried out, barely held on to her wits. While he focused on driving her crazy with his mouth, she grabbed the handcuffs, quietly fastened one to the vintage iron headboard. He stilled, looked up at her, but she didn't give him time to react. She snapped the other cuff onto his left hand.

Then she kissed her way down his chest to distract him from what she'd just done. When his eyes closed once more, she quickly climbed off him, off the bed and stepped back.

Distracting him with the promise of sex was low. No question about that, but it had been necessary.

She grabbed her bra and put it back on.

His languid expression shifted to one of wariness. "What're you doing?"

"You'll be glad I did when all this shakes down."

"What the hell?" he growled as he sat up and attempted to tug free of the headboard.

God, she had never seen that much of him. His body was pretty perfect. She almost sighed. Instead, she grabbed her tee and yanked it over her head, which she badly needed to get on straight.

"I have to go," she said, finger-combing her hair. "The sooner I lure Lorenzo's thugs away from here, the sooner you'll be safe."

"You said," he snapped, "we'd go to the sheriff in the morning."

She stuffed one foot into a sneaker and then the other. "I lied." Why pretend? He was no fool.

He yanked at the cuffs one more time. "I guess I shouldn't be surprised."

"No." She drew in a big breath. "You shouldn't. I've been lying as a way of life for a long time now. It was necessary to my existence." She turned away, couldn't bear the look in his eyes. "I'm sincerely sorry that my decision to come to Piney Woods has hurt you and others. I'm sorry you and Jodie and Dottie trusted me and were nice to me. I should never have allowed you to get so close." The emotion burning at the back of her eyes escalated her frustration. What the hell was wrong with her?

She had to be stronger than this. Smarter. Or they would all end up dead.

"So, you're just going to run." The anger in his voice was unmistakable.

"I'm not running," she argued, her ego bruised. "I'm navigating the coming storm to a different location. Away from you and the people here who I care about."

"I'm supposed to believe—" he banged a fist against his chest "—you care about me." He tugged on the handcuff again. "I can't imagine how you show your deeper feelings for a guy."

He had no idea just how deep her feelings for him went. *Big mistake, Eleanor.*

Her mother had always called her Eleanor. Only her dad and her school friends had called her Elle. That life—her real life—felt so far away. She had no one left. She'd abandoned those who hadn't died. She had thrown herself into her work and ignored all else. She had purposely chosen not to have so much as a gold-fish, much less a dog or cat. She'd had nothing and no one who could slow down what she had to do. No one and nothing that would prevent her from taking the next big risk.

One year ago, she had allowed herself to start caring again, to care about another person or thing, like sweet Raymond. Now she had to walk away.

You have to do this...have to do this.

"Disappointment you'll get over," she offered. "Dying doesn't provide that option."

She unplugged her phone, tossed it and the charger

into her backpack. She remembered the binoculars and tucked those into her backpack as well. Then she grabbed Griff's truck keys. She walked to the door, paused. As difficult as it was, she turned to face him. "I'll call Ernie in the morning and let him know you're here and in need of his assistance." She moistened her lips. "Goodbye, Griff." She started to turn away again but hesitated. "Take care of Raymond for me."

"Elle—Meg, wait."

She couldn't. She twisted the button on the knob, locking it and then closing the door behind her. He shouted after her, but she kept going, didn't want to hear his words. She stepped off the porch and slipped into the darkness.

The truck was parked behind the cabin. She took a moment to listen carefully to the night sounds. The whisper of the breeze sifting through the trees, the trickle of water in the nearby creek. The chirp of crickets, faster tonight because it was cooler. Her body adjusted to the outside temperature, to the night sounds.

The bump and clomp coming from the cabin warned her that Griff was attempting to disassemble the old iron bed. Not an easy task, and the probability of breaking it was a serious zero. It was one of the older real iron beds.

More of that regret and guilt piled on. She should go before she screwed up and changed her mind.

Going was essential. It was the only way to see with any measure of certainty that he was safe. She told herself this over and over as she moved away from the cabin and deeper into the darkness.

A soft thud down the road caused her to stop. Every muscle in her body froze. Another gentle whump.

Car door.

A good distance away. Sound carried in the dark. Her breathing slowed as her instincts elevated to a higher state of alert.

Moving slowly, listening intently, she removed her weapon from the front pouch of her backpack, then hung the backpack on her shoulder. The cold steel in her hand sent her pulse into a faster rhythm and her heart into a firmer *bump, bump.* She closed her eyes a moment and isolated the sounds she heard. Silenced the roar of blood in her ears. Ignored the thumping in her chest. Listened beyond the breeze, the trickling creek and the crickets.

A voice, possibly male. Too distant to make out the words.

Someone was here. Near the road, she thought. At least two people. She had heard the distinct sound of two different doors closing.

If there were only two, she could take them before she vanished. She had the element of surprise that they no doubt believed they possessed.

How had they learned their location?

She swore silently. Property records, of course. Ernie Battles was a friend of Griff's. Looking him up in the county database was easy peasy.

Damn it.

Moving soundlessly, she kept to the edge of the drive, near the tree line. Slowly, one careful step at a time. *Listen...listen.* The faint echo of a spoken word. Not moving closer yet.

Vague thump, then another.

Not two, four.

Her hopes sank deep into her gut, making her feel ill.

That was a risk she couldn't take. She was more likely to be overpowered by four thugs. That would leave Griff bound and vulnerable.

Meg did an about-face and moved quickly, silently back to the cabin. As soon as she hit the clearing, she leaped into a dead run. There was no time for explanations. No time to argue. She hoped like hell she could convince him without a lot of words or actions.

At the door, she turned the knob. *Damn it!* She had locked it. She wrestled with the keys on the ring with his fob. Stuck first one and then another into the lock until she had the right one. She twisted the knob again, and the door opened. She stepped inside, her finger immediately going to her lips. He had managed to drag his jeans on as well as his shoes. He stared at her now but kept his mouth shut. She grabbed his shirt from the floor and passed it to him.

"They're here," she whispered. "We have to go."

He tugged at the handcuff.

Oh hell.

She tucked her weapon into her waistband, opened the drawer, her heart pounding, and felt around inside. Where the hell was the key?

"Check the next one," he murmured.

She closed the first drawer, careful to do so quietly and then dragged open the bottom drawer. She felt around, not daring to turn on any additional lights.

Her fingers moved over something cool. Metal. She picked it up. The key. *Thank God. Thank God.*

Fingers fumbling, she fought to get the key into the slot. They were both breathing hard by the time the cuff came loose. She lowered it to the bed to prevent the clink of metal.

She pointed to the back door. Hoped like hell the trouble hadn't reached the cabin yet. She pressed her finger to her lips once more. They had to be quiet. So quiet. These people had the same training as her. They would be listening.

Her weapon in hand, she moved in the direction of the back door. She turned the knob and slowly opened the door, wishing it not to squeak. Had it squeaked when she closed it? She couldn't remember. No squeak. *Thank God.*

She stuck her head out far enough to peer around. Listened hard. No new sound, no movement.

She eased out the door. Rested each foot in the grass with care.

Griff slipped out behind her, pulled the door to without making a sound. Smart guy.

She grabbed his hand with her free one and tugged him close enough to whisper directly into his ear. "We're going into the woods. We need to go far and fast. But I don't know these woods. I need you to get us as far away from here as quickly as possible while making the least amount of sound possible."

His lips pressed against her ear. She shivered in spite of herself.

"I understand." He squeezed her hand. "Trust me. I won't let you down."

His words wrapped around her chest and squeezed. She nodded, turned her face up to his. "Lead the way."

He'd been in these woods before. Many times as a kid, he'd told her. She had no idea when he'd last hiked in the area, but he was the only shot they had of escaping.

She was counting on his recall not only to get them out of here but to get them out of here fast.

Otherwise, they were dead.

Chapter Eleven

10:15 p.m.

Griff was still buttoning his shirt as they slipped deeper into the woods. The sound of the cabin's front door being kicked in had his heart banging harder against his sternum. He wasn't sure how many there were, but he suspected more than two.

How long would it be before they realized the cabin was empty and his truck was still there?

Five, six minutes at most.

His heart rammed harder with worry. Had to get Meg out of here. He ran faster, dodging trees and clusters of shrubs in hopes of minimizing the noise from their desperate race. The stars and the moon weren't providing much in the way of light to see where the hell they were going. But the longer they were in the dark, the easier it was to see. Meg stayed close behind him. He gave himself a mental shake. Not Meg, Elle—Eleanor.

Not that it mattered what he called her. She had planned to leave him. Disappointment and no lack of hurt twisted inside him even now with trouble not far behind them.

That whole make-out session had been about getting him in a vulnerable position. The reality added anger to the emotions throttling inside him. *Damn it.*

As if she'd sensed his anger, she grabbed him by the arm and pulled him to a jarring halt. He glared at her as she leaned close. Close enough to have his body reacting as if she hadn't shown her cards already, as if he were a fool and would fall for her tricks again—and he was.

"We need to hide now," she murmured against his ear.

He forced back all those distracting emotions. Had to think a moment. The sound of air sawing in and out of his lungs had his brain struggling. Or maybe it was just her. Didn't matter. *Focus!*

Where exactly were they? He closed his eyes and pictured the area in daylight on one of those many summer days he and Ernie had played here as kids. Had prowled around like hungry bears as teenagers. The images flashed one after the other, and then he knew. There was a good hiding place nearby. It was not exactly the safest place to hide, considering snakes were on the move this time of year, but it beat the hell out of the hired guns who would be coming up right behind them any second now.

He took her hand, held it tight in his and moved more slowly, this time going westward. Whenever a twig cracked or undergrowth brushed his leg, he flinched but didn't stop. He paused at a massive tree he recognized the dark shape of, felt over the bark for the place he had carved his and Patty Hall's initials into the bark. *There.* His fingers traced the letters. A smile nudged his lips. They were close now.

He eased forward, free hand extended until he hit the outcropping of massive boulders. Large clumps of eerie grayness in the near darkness. There were all manner of stories about how the giant stones had ended up piled in this spot, but Griff wasn't sure which, if any, of those tales were true. He and Ernie had used the pile for everything from a pirate ship to a castle. He knew all the gaps between the rocks and all the hiding places beneath the overhangs of ones levered atop others.

Moving cautiously, he reached into the gap he knew provided the best cover from anyone passing by. He locked his jaw and held his breath as he felt around inside, swiping at overgrown weeds and what felt like spider webs. He encountered nothing that reacted— like a snake or raccoon or maybe a possum that might have taken refuge inside. The spot wasn't ideal for a bear or bobcat.

He tugged her closer. "Feels clear in there."

"Go," she muttered, the single syllable a frantic sound.

He climbed in, twisting his body so that he eased through the slot between rocks.

She moved in next, nestling her bottom against his lap. Not that there was any other way for two of them to fit together in the space. Then she tucked her backpack next to their legs and leaned against his chest. Instinctively, his arms went around her waist in a protective manner, despite the weapon nudging into his gut. He doubted she would appreciate the effort. She didn't need his protection. She was more than capable herself. Maybe he just needed to feel the comfort of her body in his arms.

As if he'd said out loud that her weapon was poking him, her hand slid between her back and his stomach and retrieved the weapon. A few seconds later he understood that the move hadn't been about his thoughts. The sound of undergrowth brushing fabric and boots crushing wild grass whispered across his senses.

The bad guys were close.

His arms tightened on her waist. She placed a hand on his clasped ones and squeezed reassuringly. He realized then that she had been only too glad for him to climb in first. Of course she had. That way her body shielded his. He locked his jaw and barely resisted the urge to shake his head. He should have thought of that—not that it would have done any good. She didn't take orders from him. She'd made that clear. If she had her way, she would be long gone and he'd never see her again.

For his protection.

He closed his eyes and focused on controlling his breathing. No need to allow his anger and frustration to show more than it already had. He damned sure didn't want her mistaking his tension for fear. He wasn't afraid, damn it. He blinked. Maybe he was. But not for himself. *For her.*

Given that these people from her past wanted to kill her—at least that was what she'd said, and he had no reason to believe she was lying about that aspect of all this—she would be safer if she could disappear. Rather than selfishly wanting her to stay, he should work harder to help her escape, to disappear. These scumbags would follow. No question about that. Griff and Meg were hiding in a pile of boulders with two or more armed killers tracking them like deer in open season. The intent was undeniable.

He'd been certain if she would only trust Ernie and Sheriff Norwood that they could sort this out. He'd even considered waiting until she fell asleep and using her phone to call his friend but he understood now that wasn't a gamble he was willing to take.

Urging her to stay, hoping she would, wasn't the right thing. If he wanted her safe—and he did—he should do everything in his power to help her disappear.

The reality crushed against his chest, made getting a breath nearly impossible.

The hair on the back of his neck stood on end. They were really close now. He reminded himself that unless the bad guys knew about the pile of rocks, there was no reason for them to veer in this direction. The rocks were dozens of steps in the wrong direction, in fact, back toward the cabin. He hoped these bastards assumed he and Meg were heading away from it. The clouds had shifted, so moon- and starlight were minimal. They should be okay. Yet, even knowing the trouble likely wouldn't come to the rocks, it was near enough for him to understand most of the words being muttered. A new thread of tension tightened inside him.

"They couldn't have gotten far," a man said. "Not without flashlights. It's dark as hell out here."

A crash followed by a "son of a bitch" had Griff

biting back a laugh. Someone had obviously run into a tree. The idea made him inordinately happy.

"I hate the damned woods." Female voice.

Not the Darlene woman. She was likely still in custody. Someone else.

"We should go back." Man's voice. Not the first guy who had spoken. Someone else.

Meg's body tensed noticeably. Griff's did the same. She recognized this voice, he suspected.

"If they had gone back to the cabin," the second man said, "we would've heard gunshots. Grayson has orders to shoot on sight. Trying to find them in the dark like this is an exercise in futility. We'll wait them out. They'll have to show up someplace, somewhere they feel safe, maybe with someone they can trust."

"I'm with you," the woman said.

"We'll get them," the first guy commented. "You can't cover much ground on foot in the dark in terrain like this."

Unless, Griff thought, *you know your way around.*

Their noisy departure faded as the group moved farther and farther away. Meg turned her face toward Griff's and held her finger to his lips.

He was just guessing here, but she apparently suspected the overheard conversation might be a ruse. She didn't move. He did the same. The natural night sounds enveloped the darkness once more. Now that the danger appeared to have passed—possibly—Griff wrestled with his body's reaction to her butt being pressed into his lap. He thought about the animals back at his place. He thought about the video he'd watched of her slicing that guy's throat. None of it alleviated the situation. His body just kept hardening.

He was on the verge of going over the edge, and if she moved, that would be the end of his control for sure.

Rustling grass snapped his thoughts away from the tension building between them.

The beam of a flashlight flickered in the trees.

Griff held his breath.

She had been right to wait. At least one of them was still out there.

The light danced over the rocks.

Holy hell.

The threat moved closer. Grass crushed under footfalls. Fabric rustled against fabric. The beam of light skipped over their location, thankfully not pausing long enough to reveal the crevice in which they remained packed like sardines.

He or she—probably *he*, judging by the sound of the footfalls—made their way around the small mountain of large rocks, pausing here and there and shining the light into gaps. Slowly, the person reached all the way around to where they'd begun. The light bounced over their location again.

Griff's breath stalled in his lungs.

The light shifted back, landed right next to his shoulder, then after five frantic thumps in his chest, it moved on.

Footfalls faded as the person walked away.

Griff managed a breath. The bastard had missed them.

The minutes ticked past, and still Meg made no move to emerge from their hiding place. He was in no hurry either. At this point, he would be a fool not to trust her instincts. She clearly knew her way around this sort of situation.

Finally, she leaned forward and poked her upper body between the rocks. Then she eased all the way out.

Griff's legs had gone numb, and other parts of him remained stiff and at full attention. It took a minute, but he managed to get up and thread his body through the opening as well. Not nearly as gracefully as she had, but he got out all the same.

She moved in close to him again, whispered against his ear, making his body tingle despite the gravity of the situation. *Damn.* He had to get a hold of himself.

She said, "We need to go back to the road, around the cabin where we can see but they can't. Can you find the way?"

He nodded.

She tugged her backpack on her shoulder once more, tucked her weapon into her waistband at the front this time and reached for his hand.

He closed his around hers, and his heart clutched. He wanted desperately to keep her safe, but she sure as hell appeared better at this than he would be. He'd have to follow her lead on that part. But he knew the woods, and that would be his contribution to saving their lives.

MEG HELD TIGHTLY to Griff's hand as he started the slow, laborious process of moving soundlessly through the woods. She followed his steps precisely to avoid bigger clumps of wild grass and underbrush. Not to mention trees. It was so dark. Even though her eyes had adjusted well enough, it was still like walking blindfolded. The clouds had moved in, blocking the meager moon- and starlight. Probably had saved their lives back there. She sure as hell wasn't going to complain now.

The air was crisp at this hour. She couldn't be certain what time it was, but she estimated around midnight.

She struggled to stay focused on getting out of here. The struggle lay in the voice she had heard back there while tucked into that rock crevice.

His.

She would know that voice anywhere, anytime.

Kase Ridley. They had worked together off and on over the years. Had been on-again-off-again lovers. Friends. Or at least she'd thought so. Then he'd disappeared on an operation, and she'd been sent in to find him—dead or alive. But she hadn't found him. All she'd found was serious trouble, trouble that almost got her killed, and then she'd had no choice but to disappear.

Now she understood. He was alive. And he was working for the other side.

Fury roared inside her, but she had to push it down. Getting the hell out of here alive was all that mattered just now. She would deal with the Ridley issue later.

The progress was slow on the route Griff had chosen since the trees were thicker, which meant the undergrowth was as well. Occasionally she caught a glimpse of the cabin light, so they weren't far from their destination. She was immensely grateful for Griff's ability to navigate these woods.

They moved beyond the cabin close enough to hear the sound of voices. The four remained gathered there. Likely looking for any clues that might suggest where she and Griff had headed next. One of the scumbags was going through Griff's truck. Another stood by and watched the search or kept a lookout. The other two were inside ransacking the cabin by the sound of it.

Griff moved faster now and she was glad. They needed a certain level of a head start when they reached the vehicles the thugs had left at the road. It would be fairly easy to call one of Griff's friends to pick them up, but that would only draw someone else into this mess. Calling an Uber or other hired car would waste too much valuable time and put those drivers at risk too.

When they cleared the tree line and started toward the road, Meg broke away from him and ran. There were two sedans. Both black of course. Hopefully at least one was unlocked.

Not the first one. *Damn it.* She dug her knife from her backpack and passed it to Griff. "Take care of the tires," she murmured.

He gave a nod and set to work on her request.

The driver side door on the second one opened. Meg smiled. The fob lay in a cupholder. "Sloppy," she murmured as she slid in.

Griff rushed around the trunk of the second vehicle and dropped into the passenger seat. Ensuring the exterior lights were off, she started the engine and eased backward along the narrow gravel drive until she was on the pavement, then she cut the wheel and drifted out onto the road. Once she was on the road, she gave it some gas. Not enough to squeal tires but enough to get moving in a hurry.

She drove a mile or so before turning on the headlights.

"What now?" he asked.

"I have a backup vehicle in a storage unit. We pick it up and dump this car."

"Sounds like you thought of everything."

Not everything, or she wouldn't have been caught off guard by the voice she'd heard in those woods. Not all that she should have, considering Griff was with her. She glanced at him; his profile was set in stone, his beard-shadowed jaw tense. She could just imagine the thoughts going through his head. None of which would be good.

Just drive.

She focused forward and drove as fast as she dared until she hit the main road, and even then she was careful. Getting pulled over would not be a good thing by any stretch of the imagination. She couldn't afford the wasted time or the potential that Ernie had put out a BOLO for them. The one thing that would keep them alive with any certainty was staying a step ahead of the thugs Lorenzo had sent.

She blinked at the idea that Ridley was one of them.

Was it possible he was undercover? That he really wasn't one of *them*?

No. He'd said they had orders to shoot on sight.

Would he have shot her? Killed her?

She shuddered inside. Every instinct she possessed warned he would have.

Taking the back roads to her destination, she surveyed the dark houses. The world was sleeping. They had no idea that killers were so close, that there were people—like her and Griff—who were running for their lives. Running right past the homes where they slept. Wouldn't it be nice to enjoy the sleep of ignorant bliss? Sure, the news could be scary, but the news never told the whole story. The stories about those who sacrificed their lives to find the whole truth, to bring down the worst of the worst. The stories that no one ever heard.

The stories of those who could never be honored for their heroism. Never be publicly thanked for what they had sacrificed.

Didn't matter, people like her didn't do it for the shiny awards or the kudos. They did it to see the bad guys pay for their evil deeds. To see that justice was served—no matter the cost required to make that happen.

"You okay?"

The sound of Griff's voice startled her from the unfortunate musings. "Yeah. You?"

"I'm good."

She smiled as she thought of the way his body had responded to hers while they were stuffed between those rocks. She had longed to shift around to face him, straddling him in a way that pressed her more intimately to him. Part of her wished now that she'd acted on the attraction that had sparked between them from the very beginning. But she had known that getting so close wouldn't be a good idea. Wasn't one now. Still, she was only human. She had needs. Needs that had been ignored for about two years now.

They drove the rest of the way to the destination in

silence. She wasn't looking forward to any questions he might have, and the more they talked, the more likely he was to ask things she didn't want to answer.

The storage facility office was closed, but there was twenty-four-hour access to the units. She pulled up the gate, entered the code and it opened. She drove through and worked her way along the maze of units until she reached the one that was hers. The units for storing vehicles were at the back and were set a broader distance apart from the others to facilitate pulling in and out. She parked the car to the left side of the door and grabbed the fob as she emerged. Not that she didn't trust Griff, but on some level, he had to be afraid of what would happen next. Fear made people do desperate, generally unwise things. She didn't want him making a mistake.

She entered the code for the unit and raised the door. The small SUV waited, full of gas and with a trickle charger to keep the battery fully operational. She removed the charger, closed the hood and climbed in. The car started without hesitation. She eased it from the unit and parked it to the far right of the door.

She backed up the stolen car and then pulled it into the unit. She then closed the door and set the locking system. Good to go.

Griff followed her to the SUV she'd had stored and climbed into the passenger seat.

When she'd driven out of the facility, he asked, "What now?"

"We find a place to lay low and figure that out."

She eased along the dark street. Breathing unhindered for the first time in hours.

"You recognized one of those guys."

It wasn't a question. He'd likely felt the tension in her body. The unexpected shock had disabled her ability to hide her response to the voice she hadn't heard in two years.

"I did."

"Was it someone you worked with before, when you were Angela Hamilton?"

"Yes."

"Is he the reason you're on the run?"

Meg drove for a bit before figuring out the best way to answer without revealing too much. "In part."

"Was he more than a colleague?"

The change in his tone told her he hadn't wanted to ask that question but hadn't been able to stop himself. She should be flattered that he was jealous, obviously. But what she felt was fear. Jealousy was the kind of emotion that got a person into trouble faster than most others.

"Sometimes."

Griff stared out the window at the closed shops of downtown Chattanooga.

"Sometimes," she went on, deciding it would be better to assuage whatever he was feeling than to allow it to smolder, "when you're deep into an operation and everyone around you is the enemy, you grab onto the only one who is in the same boat as you."

"He's one of the good guys?" He didn't attempt to conceal his doubt.

"When I knew him, he was." Obviously, that had changed.

"If you can no longer trust him, is there anyone in your old life you can trust?"

That was the problem. She couldn't be sure.

"I wish I knew the answer. But I don't. I'm on my own here, and I'll just have to wing it until I see some other way."

"You've still got me."

The words were spoken in such a heartfelt manner she could hardly breathe. Griff really meant what he said. But it was the biggest mistake of all. If only she could make him see that.

"I appreciate that you still want to help after all that's happened," she said carefully. "But helping me has already put you in grave danger. Has caused you serious trouble. They now recognize that you're with me because you want to be and not because I'm forcing you. That's a dangerous place to put yourself in all this."

He stared straight ahead into the night, his jaw working with mounting tension. "I'll take my chances."

"Everyone loves a hero, Griff." Meg drew in a breath. "Except the family and friends he leaves behind to grieve the loss."

"But what would the world do without heroes?"

He stared at her profile. He wanted an answer. Wanted her to look him in the eyes. She wasn't sure he was going to like the answer she had to give.

She braked for a red traffic light and turned to him, looked directly into his eyes. "Don't be a hero for me, Griff. Save it for someone who actually deserves it."

Chapter Twelve

Givens Road
Chattanooga, Tennessee
Tuesday, May 7, 1:18 a.m.

It was late—or early depending on the way you looked at it—when Meg reached the address she'd found on Zillow. The house had been on the market for several months, and it was empty. More importantly, the neighbors weren't terribly close, and the acre and a half lot was thickly treed, providing lots of privacy.

She drove around behind the house and parked, shut off the engine and reached for the door handle.

"You're really going to break into this house?" He stared at her in the darkness.

He'd watched her kill another human being, twice, and shoot yet another. Not to mention the ass-kicking she'd given the two hooligans who'd showed up at her shop. And he was worried about her breaking into a house?

"I'm borrowing it for the night. If anyone stops by, we're giving it a test run to see if we like it."

He exhaled a big breath. "Okay."

Yeah. Okay. She got out, grabbed her backpack and

the bag of stuff she kept in her backup vehicle. Toiletries, a couple changes of clothes. Snacks, bottled water. Preparation was key to most all aspects of survival. Her former boss had drilled that concept into her head. *Never get caught without a backup plan. Never get weighed down by extra baggage.*

Her gaze settled on Griff. She surely botched that last one.

He took the extra bag from her, made a face at the weight of it. "What've you got in here? Ammunition?"

"Stuff we'll need," she said as she considered the best way to enter the house.

First, she walked around with a flashlight (a handy tool also stored in the backup vehicle) and checked for a security system. The media cable was shut off. No sign of a landline. No other wires that shouted security system. So unless there was a wireless one, they were good to go on getting in without any trouble.

The back door had a dead bolt, but it wasn't engaged, so picking the lock was a piece of cake. The door led directly into the kitchen area. Griff shook his head at this new skill of hers as well. She didn't see how that could lower his opinion of her any farther than it was already.

First thing, she did a walk through and scanned for wireless security products. Nothing.

"We're good," she said, coming back to where he waited by the back door. She locked the door and engaged the dead bolt as the last real estate agent who'd visited should have.

Griff placed the bag he'd been holding on the counter. Meg turned on the light above the kitchen sink since it was at the back of the house and less likely to be noticed. Not that she believed anyone could see the house from the street. It was well concealed.

She shifted her attention to her not completely reluctant hostage. "You want to shower first? I have a phone call I need to make."

He shrugged. "Sure." He tugged at his shirt. "I don't have any other clothes, but a shower will definitely help."

She picked through the bag on the counter and handed him shampoo and body wash, along with a towel. "That's the only towel, so hang it up when you're done. I'll be using it too."

He hesitated before going in search of the one bathroom the house had according to the real estate listing. "Who are you calling? Ernie?"

"The less Ernie knows, the safer we are. So, no, I'm not calling Ernie. I'm calling my former boss." She hadn't spoken to him since the day she disappeared. She wasn't so sure that talking to him now was the right move, but it was the only one she had left under the circumstances. She hoped something else came to mind soon, but not so far.

That wasn't entirely true. She shouldn't lie to herself that way. There were others she could call, but she needed to give this man the benefit of the doubt. He'd taught her everything she knew. Treated her like a daughter after her own father passed away. He'd been her rock before everything fell apart.

But something was off and she couldn't fit the pieces together. Nothing new really. She'd known there was a glitch somewhere fifteen months ago which was why she'd chosen to take herself out of the scenario rather than allowing someone else to reset her.

Now, more than a year later, it was looking like she had made the right decision.

"Can he—your former boss," Griff asked, "help you out of this situation?"

The simple answer was yes. He could extract her. Direct her to a safe house until she could be debriefed. But there had to be trust involved to allow someone that sort of power. She'd lost trust fifteen months ago. Had she been premature in her decision back then? Maybe. But at least she was alive. That was a hell of a lot better than the alternative.

"I'm not sure." She met his expectant gaze and decided to tell him the truth. "I always trusted him before, but something happened that shook my confidence in the whole system. It's possible he wasn't part of the problem. That possibility is the reason I'm going to call him."

Griff nodded as if he got it. "You're giving him an opportunity to prove himself."

"I am."

"And if he doesn't come through?"

"Then I'll know I made the right decision fifteen months ago, and I'll understand that I'm on my own now."

He held her gaze for a long moment, searching, assessing. Maybe looking for something to give him the answer he needed. Finally, he said, "I'm sorry you were let down before. I hope he doesn't let you down this time."

With that, he slung the one towel over his shoulder

and went in search of the bathroom. It hadn't crossed her mind that she might need two towels. She hadn't expected to ever trust anyone again. What was it about this man that made her want to trust him? To lean into him? To be with him?

Didn't matter. Her needs could get him killed and she couldn't live with that.

When she heard the water running, she steeled herself and pulled out her cell. She entered the number she knew by heart, waited through three rings.

"Who is this and how did you get this number?"

The voice—the one that had always had the power to steady her—shook her now. She hesitated. Focused on calming the pounding in her chest. She wrestled the emotions aside. "Agent 16578 reporting in"

"Eleanor?"

"No one else has that number," she pointed out. "And I'm reasonably confident not too many people have your private cell number."

"Where the hell are you? We thought you were dead."

"It doesn't matter where I am right now." She watched the time. "What matters is that we have a situation. Our comrade Kase Ridley is working for the other side."

"What? That's impossible. Eleanor, you need to come in. We've ironed out the issues from that day. You have been exonerated completely. There is nothing to fear."

She refused to be swayed by the words that a year ago she would have given her right arm to hear. "I don't have a lot of time. You need to call Ridley back in. He's working for Lorenzo."

"Just tell me where you are, Eleanor. Let me help you."

His continued evasion of her statement set her further on edge.

"Don't ignore my warning," she reiterated. Then she ended the call. She struggled to slow her pounding heart. Forced her respiration to steady.

Then, for a bit, she replayed the brief conversation. The surprise in his voice had been real enough. He hadn't expected to hear from her. He really had thought she was dead. And he insisted it was impossible that Ridley had gone to the dark side.

This was not good, she decided. On second thought, she decided the surprise wasn't real in terms of her being alive; it was about her calling him. She had been trained far too well, had never failed in an assignment. She wouldn't be taken down so easily. So the surprise was that he hadn't expected her to call him. Which might mean that he was aware of what Ridley was doing. Was that an indication that Ridley was acting with the sanction of the chain of command?

Her gut said yes.

Deputy Director Arthur Wisting would know if he'd lost an operative to the other side. He was far too astute to be caught off guard so easily.

Which meant she was screwed.

If she couldn't trust her old boss—certainly couldn't trust Ridley—then who could she trust? How far up the chain did this go?

Worse—sadly, it did get worse—this meant that she could not be allowed to survive under any circumstances.

She started to pace. This was why Ridley was involved. He knew her better than anyone. He would be the best option for eliminating her.

If Wisting had known she was alive all this time and didn't actively attempt to find her, then maybe he'd been willing to let her go, but now that had changed. She knew their secret. Ridley, perhaps with Wisting's blessing, was no longer on the right side.

Okay, all she had to do was disappear before they found her. No problem. She'd done it before, she could do it again. Though it was true that Ridley knew her better than anyone else save perhaps Wisting himself, she also knew Ridley. He was as vulnerable as she was.

Determination filled her. She wasn't going down easy.

The water in the shower stopped. She glanced in the direction of the bathroom. The one glitch in her plan was Griff. How did she protect him? Ridley would use Griff against her to manipulate her. It was Undercover 101. Learn the enemy's weaknesses and use them against him.

At this very moment, Ernie, Jodie and Dottie were in danger as well. But Griff would be the one Ridley zeroed in on. Meg knew how he thought. Going after Griff was the step she would take, if the circumstances were reversed. Ridley would quickly determine which of those people around her were the highest-value target. The fact that Griff was on the run with her would elevate his worth many times over.

A good friend would listen to your sob story, your issues, your mistakes, but a best friend—the closest friend—would show up with a shovel to help bury the problem.

She had to find a way to take Griff out of the line of fire.

GRIFF RUBBED THE towel over his skin. He hadn't heard much of Meg's conversation, but what little he had didn't sound good. She was in real trouble. He desperately wished he could make her understand that she had friends here. The past didn't matter. Ernie would help. Sheriff Norwood would go with whatever Ernie suggested. Loads of other people would be more than glad to throw in their support.

But Meg wouldn't take the risk.

It wasn't for her own safety that she ignored this option. She was doing it to protect him and the people she considered friends.

How did he convince her that she was looking at this all wrong?

He swiped his palm over the foggy mirror and then finger-combed his hair. Rubbing a hand over his jaw, he realized he needed a shave far more badly than he'd realized. But grooming had been the furthest thing from his mind for the past twenty-four or so hours. Staying alive and making sure Meg stayed that way too was priority one.

Not that she wasn't damned good at taking care of herself. Her skill with a weapon—hell, in hand-to-hand combat even—was stellar. Like nothing he'd ever seen in real life. In the movies, yeah, but not in what he'd thought to be an everyday person. The real problem was, in his opinion, if she was so busy keeping everyone else safe, she might fall down on the job of protecting herself. He intended to ensure that didn't happen.

He hung the towel over the shower curtain rod and pulled on his already worn clothes. By daylight, it would be necessary for them to move, so he had until then to convince her that she should accept help from him and the people who cared about her. As smart as she was, she would see through his attempts if he pushed too hard.

Griff opened the bathroom door and walked out, determined to do whatever was necessary to convince her to trust him, to work with him before going out on her own. She stood in the kitchen near the sink eating a protein bar. He smiled, couldn't help himself. She looked so young and vulnerable in that dim light.

He almost laughed at the thought. Young, she was. Vulnerable, not so much.

"The shower's all yours," he announced. As tired as he was, he felt a little better after his. All things considered, he supposed part of it was simply being thankful that they were both still alive.

She finished off the bar, tossed the wrapper on the counter. "Turn off this light and keep a watch out the windows while I'm in there, will you?"

He nodded. "You worried they've found us already?"

"Nope. Just want to make sure none of the neighbors who might be out for a nightly walk notice activity in here and nose around."

"I can do that." He reached out and flipped off the light, leaving them in total darkness.

She took a slug of water. "Thanks."

"What about your phone?" he asked. "You threw mine away—I'm assuming so it couldn't be traced. What about yours?"

"There are ways to prevent a cell phone from being traced. I've made a point of knowing them all."

With that she walked away. The sound of her bare feet padding across the wood floor had him following the vague outline of her body in the darkness. He loved the shape of her, the smell of her—even after huddling in a pile of rocks for what felt like hours and plowing through the woods for endless minutes. There was a sweetness about her skin. She tasted so good. Not to mention she was seriously hot to look at.

How many times had he covertly analyzed her long toned legs and licked his lips while tracing her hips or her breasts with his gaze. It was a miracle she hadn't caught him eyeing her like that. Several of his friends had mentioned how gorgeous she was. The best part about it was that she didn't seem to even notice how good she looked. All she had to do was glance in the mirror, but apparently she didn't see herself that way. She was just who she was. Good-natured. Kind. Sweet.

He shook his head. Sweet? Actually, what she was, was badass. He grinned. Seriously badass.

When the water started to run, he decided to do something she wouldn't appreciate if she caught him. He opened her backpack and had a look inside. He found two passports. One under the name Eleanor Holt. In the picture, her hair was darker and she looked younger. The next passport was under the name Elle

Longwood. The photo in this one was Meg with her usual dark hair but lighter than in the other photo.

There was a wad of cash. Drivers licenses under the same names as the passports. Keys to what looked like lockboxes and maybe houses. Another smaller handgun. Snacks, bottles of water.

Who was Eleanor Holt? Was Holt actually her last name? What kind of operation had she been working on when things went south and she had to disappear? Who was this guy whose voice she recognized? Had he been a partner? Colleague? Lover? She'd indicated yes to all three, but was she telling Griff what he expected to hear? He had learned that about her. Maybe it was some kind of psychology move. Tell a person what they want to hear and they stop asking questions.

The water shut off, and he remembered she'd asked him to keep watch on the windows.

Feeling like as ass, he moved from window to window and surveyed the dark yard and trees. No movement. No sound. He confirmed that both the front and back doors were locked. Then he went back to the kitchen and grabbed a protein bar. He had no idea what time it was. The digital clocks on the stove and the microwave flashed midnight as if there had been a power outage at some point and no one had bothered to set them. The last time he'd looked at the clock in the SUV, it had been after midnight, so it had to be one or well past that by now.

If any of the events had hit the news, Griff's mom and sister would be beside themselves. He should call his mom and let her know he was okay. Maybe Meg would let him call since her cell was untraceable.

Considering how tough Meg was, she might not see him wanting to call his mother as very manly or strong.

But he had the perfect excuse. He loved his mother and he didn't want her to worry. He thought he knew Meg well enough to believe she would feel the same way if her parents were still alive. Had all the talk about her parents been lies? She had said it was all true…

The bathroom door opened, and he turned in that direction, pondering the fact that she was all alone in this world and that circumstance had perhaps nudged her toward such a risky career. Except she had him and the other people in Piney Woods who adored her. She didn't have to do that anymore. Would driving that detail home help her to see that she didn't need to run? They could fight this battle together.

She rubbed her hair with the towel to dry it since there was no hair dryer. "All clear?"

"All clear." His eyes had adjusted to the darkness so that he could just make out her form and a little of her face.

"We should get some sleep," she said. "There's a rug in the living room but not much elsewhere except the hardwood floor."

"Works for me."

She picked up her backpack and walked in that direction. He followed. She dropped her bag on the rug and sat down next to it, still working on her hair. He settled on the rug on the opposite side. He searched his brain for a way to kick off the conversation they needed to have, but nothing readily bobbed to the surface. Maybe he was just too tired to sort this out.

"I've been thinking," she said, her voice softer than usual.

Since they weren't worried about anyone overhearing them, her quiet tone had him coming to fuller attention. "Me too," he confessed.

She said nothing for a few seconds, then, "You go first."

Frustration thumped him. He shouldn't have said anything. He should have just let her go on. There was no taking it back now. He drew in a big breath. *Just say it.* "I think you underestimate how many friends you have in Piney Woods. We'll band together and help you if you'll only let us."

She laughed softly. Sighed. The laugh part worried him.

"I'm going to tell you everything," she said. "I think it will help you see how what you're suggesting won't work."

When he would have argued, she added, "Not that I don't appreciate the offer, and I do know that I have many friends in Piney Woods. I am very grateful for all of you."

"Then let us help you." The sound of her voice in the darkness had his body reacting. *Come on, Griff, get your head in the right place.*

"First," she said as she tossed the towel and stretched out on her side to face him, "let me tell you what I'm up against."

He opted not to correct her, but it was what *they* were up against. He lay down on the rug facing her, a safe distance between them. *No pushing*, he reminded himself.

"I joined the LAPD right out of USC—the University of Southern California. I went to the academy and rose to detective in record time. Then four years ago, I was approached by a man who was putting together a special team of operatives composed of police detectives, DEA and FBI agents. It was to be the first of its kind. He selected members of law enforcement who had excelled in their fields. He vetted hundreds of people. When he selected his group, the team's first mission was to go after the biggest drug lord on the West Coast, Salvadori Lorenzo."

"I don't know the name." Griff hated admitting this, but it was true. No point pretending. If she wanted to tell him the story, he wanted the whole story. He needed it.

"I'm not surprised. He isn't exactly a household name. The average Californian thinks he's just another billionaire who lives in Beverly Hills and donates to all the right causes and parties. But people in the higher echelons of law enforcement on the West Coast know who he is. He is the primary connection in this country to one of Mexico's most notorious drug cartels. When he says jump, even the top member of that cartel asks how high on the way up. He is untouchable."

"Your job was to infiltrate his business," he surmised. Griff knew it. She wasn't a killer. She was a cop. An undercover cop. A smile tugged at his mouth, and he wanted to reach over and hug her hard.

"Not in the beginning. I had other operations. It

wasn't until things went sour with the operative we had inside Lorenzo's clique."

"Let me guess," Griff offered, "the man whose voice you heard in the woods back there."

"The one and only. Kase Ridley."

"This drew you into Lorenzo's world." Griff got it now.

"It did. My boss, Arthur Wisting, set up my profile, Angela Hamilton, assassin for hire. My first step toward breaking into his tight little group was going after one of his men who'd stepped over a certain line. Lorenzo was so impressed by my courage that he hired me on the spot. It all went down exactly as Wisting had hoped."

She really was fearless. *Damn.* "You actually went after one of his men?"

"I did. It was do or die. I tap-danced my way into his good graces, and he became quite fond of me during the months that followed."

Griff wanted to ask if she'd had to kill anyone to prove herself, but he wanted her to keep talking, and that question might just shut this moment down.

"Things were rocking along exactly as planned until Ridley got himself into a no-win situation, and I was ordered to extract him."

He waited for her to go on, the urge to reach out and give her arm a squeeze of reassurance nearly overwhelming, but again, he didn't want to stop the momentum.

"During the attempted extraction, Lorenzo's one and only son was killed. He believes I killed him."

Damn. "How old was this son?" He felt confident they weren't talking about a child.

"Twenty-nine-year-old piece of garbage who got off on watching people die. Do I feel guilty that he's dead?" She laughed. "No way. The world is a better place without him."

"Wait," Griff said, replaying what she'd said, "Lorenzo believes you killed his son. Did you?"

"It doesn't matter. He's dead and Lorenzo wants me dead."

Griff had a feeling there was more to it. "The Ridley guy just let you take the fall either way."

"He was in deeper. It was better that I took the fall. Except then he disappeared, was presumed dead—until now."

"Wait." Griff held up his hands. "Didn't they offer to protect you?"

"Sure." She made a sound, a scoff. "Do you know how many cops survive in witness protection? I wouldn't have stood a chance against Lorenzo's reach. Case in point, Ernie runs my prints and less than twenty-four hours later Lorenzo has people right here in Piney Woods. He has ears everywhere. I knew my only choice was to disappear completely without any help from anyone."

Griff finally understood. Meg had been right. She would never be safe unless she disappeared, leaving no trace and no one who knew.

"I'm sorry I didn't understand." She had the weight of all this on her shoulders, and she'd been carrying it alone all this time.

She sighed. "I guess you kind of had to be there."

He reached over, took her hand. He held it gently. Wishing there was more he could do. More he could say.

Her mouth was suddenly on his. She kissed him with such urgency, such need. He didn't resist. He understood. She needed him in the only way he could help right now.

And he intended to give her everything she wanted.

Chapter Thirteen

Givens Road
Chattanooga, Tennessee
6:00 a.m.

Meg watched Griff sleep. As much as she understood this thing with him had been a mistake, she couldn't really see it that way. She had never been in love. Ever. She had dearly loved her parents. She'd cared very much for friends and even some work colleagues. But she had never been the textbook definition of "in love."

Despite her lack of experience in the area, she felt confident this feeling that sizzled between her and Griff was exactly that—being in love. She wanted desperately to spend time with him, to simply be with him. She had never been a social butterfly. She'd had no long or impressive list of boyfriends or lovers. She had always been more focused on education and then work. Filling her social calendar or satisfying her physical needs had never been at the top of her agenda. Never a high priority. There were far too many other things that took precedence.

She and Griff had enjoyed each other's bodies until

exhaustion had overtaken them just before sunrise. He'd fallen asleep while she showered again, and she was glad. She'd wanted to just sit and look at him. To watch him breathe. To study his face and his naked body in the morning light.

He was the nicest and kindest man she had ever met. Before Griff, her father had held that standing. He had been her idol. Her father had known how to treat a woman. He had respected and supported her mother. Always backed her up. Always stood at her side. Even as a little girl, she had known this was the kind of man she wanted to fall in love with one day.

And here he was, but the timing could not be worse.

How was she supposed to follow her heart? To pursue this love she had found? She couldn't if she wanted to protect him from the trouble that had descended upon this new life she had created.

She was out of options. The smart thing to do would be to leave now before he woke. She could write to him later and explain how difficult the decision had been. He wouldn't understand, but at least he would be alive.

Except the only way that worked was if she turned herself over to Lorenzo. They had connected Griff to her, and they would use him against her. If hers and Ridley's positions were reversed, she would do the same. To win, being heartless was by far the better position of strength.

She stood, rounded up her backpack. She had already dressed in the one change of clothes she'd had. Creeping through the house, headed for the front door, she forced herself to keep staring forward.

Don't look back.

"Are you leaving?"

Without me, he didn't bother to add. The answer was obvious.

She stalled at the front door, squeezed her eyes shut for a moment. Deep breath. She braced herself and turned to face him. That he stood there dragging on his jeans did nothing to make this any easier. From his sleep-tousled hair to his bare feet, he was as sexy as hell. The way he looked at her, disappointed and at once hopeful made her feel a level of regret she couldn't pretend away.

"Leaving is the one step I can take that will protect you and everyone else here who I mistakenly allowed to get close to me. I just can't risk what might happen to one or all of you by staying."

Griff braced his hands on his lean hips. That he had left his jeans unfastened made her want to sigh. Made her hungry for more of what they'd shared in the wee hours of the morning.

"What you're saying," he suggested, "is that if you leave—run away—we'll all be safe because you're gone. These thugs will just leave, probably in an effort to pick up your trail."

He knew she wasn't saying that. "They will leave when I leave because I will give them my location."

His lips tightened. She watched, vividly remembering the feel of those lips on her skin, on every part of her.

"You're going to sacrifice yourself to protect me and the others." He shook his head. "Doesn't sound all that smart to me. Based on your actions so far, I was expecting a far more ingenious plan. This one sounds a little like the easy way out."

"Less complicated," she agreed. "Not so much easier."

She would not sacrifice him or anyone else who'd had the misfortune of landing in her path to save herself. No way.

He stepped closer. She had trouble drawing a breath.

"All right then. If you have to go, then I'm going with you."

Damn it. What part of this did he not understand? "You can't do that."

"Why not?" His chin went up in defiance.

"Think about your family. Your mother. Your sister and her family. The animals. All those dogs, cats, horses...chickens." She shrugged. "They're all depending on you. You can't just walk away."

"Lonnie will see that the animals are taken care of," he argued. "I'll find a way to see my family when I can."

He was serious.

"Griff." She exhaled a weary breath, felt suddenly exhausted all over again. "This is on me. I have to handle it. I promise you that if I can find a way to come back, I will. But you cannot be involved in what happens today."

"If," he echoed, "you know they'll kill you, then there's no coming back."

The tremor in his voice as he said the words ripped her apart inside. "They've tried before." She forced an exaggerated smile and a lackluster shrug. "Killing me isn't as easy as they'd like it to be."

"If I can't talk you into staying," he said, "then at least let me help you."

How could he be that sweet, that willing to sacrifice himself to help her? He could not be that dense. He surely understood that to go with her was pure suicide.

"I'm willing to listen to what you believe you can do to help." It was the least she could do. He deserved her respect even if she would never agree to whatever he suggested.

Her tone no doubt conveyed the lack of confidence she had in the possibility that he or anyone could help her.

"We set a trap," he offered, "lure them in using the two of us as bait."

"We could do that," she agreed. "If we're lucky, we could take down Ridley and his crew."

"Then why aren't we planning that move right now?" He turned his hands up in question. "It makes sense."

It did. To a point. Good men like Griff believed in standing on the side of right. Of fighting for truth and fairness. He couldn't fathom the depths of depravity to which someone like Lorenzo would go. "Here's the sticking point in your plan. Lorenzo will send someone else and then someone after that. He will keep sending hired killers to take me and anyone close to me out until the job is done."

Griff turned his hands up, clearly out of suggestions. "Then we go after him."

That wasn't a suggestion; that was a death sentence.

"Many have tried," she said with a genuine note of

sadness. "All have failed. They either end up dead or working for him."

He looked away. "I guess that's a good enough reason to simply give up and let him win."

Now he was just trying to anger her. "There are some wars that can't be won." She couldn't keep doing this. "Goodbye, Griff."

She turned back to the door.

Her cell vibrated. She started to ignore it. To wait until she was in the SUV and driving away to check the screen, but some deeply honed instinct warned that she shouldn't miss this call.

She pulled it from her back pocket and checked the screen. Not a number she recognized. She hit Accept and pressed the device to her ear. "Yeah."

"Long time no see."

Ridley.

"Not long enough." Why sugarcoat it? He was one of them now.

He chuckled; the sound held no amusement. "Look, I'll cut to the chase."

"Please do, I have places to go." Except she had a feeling her travel itinerary was about to change dramatically. "You know, I talked to the boss about you. He was surprised to hear you were working for the other side now."

"You see, Elle, that's what happens when you stay out of the loop for too long. Things change. Maybe the boss didn't mention it, but he works on this side too. He doesn't like to talk about how the government has left him needing to plump up his personal retirement plan. You just can't rely on anything anymore."

Why wasn't she surprised? "You can't trust any-one either."

"No," he agreed, "you cannot. Speaking of which, several of your friends and I are having breakfast at the diner in this quaint little town you've been holed up in. We'd like you to join us, oh say, no later than eight thirty."

Equal measures of fear and fury roared through her veins. "You know me, Rid," she shot back, keeping all that fear and fury out of her voice, "I don't have any friends."

"Let's see," he mused, "we have Jodie."

A squeal told Meg he'd nudged Jodie with his weapon or made some other thuggish move. Meg grit-ted her teeth to hold back a reaction.

"Dottie."

Another yelp.

Meg flinched.

"There are half a dozen others sitting around wait-ing for breakfast. Including Deputy Battles and one of his little minions. I'd hate to see anyone get hurt, but you know how the boys I hang with can be some-times. Oh wait, I should mention that the two depu-ties are a little worse for wear, but not to worry. It's nothing a good ER doc can't fix. Assuming they ar-rive in a timely fashion."

Her rage mounted, searing away the fear. There were things she wanted to say to him. No, actually she wanted to shove her weapon into his mouth and blow his head off. That would make her immensely happy. But chances were, she would never get the op-portunity. Not now.

She smiled sadly. This was the life she'd chosen. The one that had made her feel as if she were making a difference. Too late to regret those decisions now.

She glanced at Griff. Too late for a lot of things.

"I'll be there," she assured him. "By eight thirty."

She ended the call. Stared at the screen for a long moment.

"Wherever you're going," Griff said as he tugged on a shoe, "I'm going too."

He'd already pulled on his shirt. As she watched, her ability to relay the gist of the conversation suddenly unavailable, he slipped on the other shoe, then stuffed the tail of his shirt into the waistband of his jeans.

"Where are we going?" he asked, moving closer.

She cleared her throat, somehow found her voice. "That was Ridley. He has Jodie and Dottie and Ernie. Some others too. At the diner. He and his pals are holding them hostage until I show up."

The look on Griff's face lanced her heart. He understood just how bad this was.

"I'm calling Sheriff Norwood."

Meg wanted to tell him it wouldn't matter, but why bother? The debate would only waste time.

Griff held out his hand and she placed her cell phone there. He made the call and talked to the sheriff, giving her a quick overview of their state of affairs.

Meg listened to the way he framed the situation, to the things he said about her. The way he described Meg as a hero in need of backup. Her throat tightened; her heart expanded, making it impossible to breathe.

His words reminded her of something she'd almost

allowed herself to forget: you could be down or you could be beaten. As long as you were still breathing, the choice was your own.

She smiled. She was down for sure, but she damned well was not beaten.

She had one potential ace up her sleeve. Making that call was a risk. A damned huge risk, but it was better than going down without a fighting chance. She knew the whole truth now. Maybe it was time someone else did as well.

Maybe it would help, maybe it wouldn't. Either way, distraction always provided opportunity. Whether it kept them alive or not was yet to be seen.

Chapter Fourteen

Pampered Paws
Pine Boulevard
Piney Woods, Tennessee
8:05 a.m.

"I don't like the idea of you going in there alone,"
Sheriff Norwood said.

Griff didn't like it either. "They know I'm with you,"
he tossed in. "Why wouldn't they expect me to be
with you?"

"At this point," Meg argued, "any and all things
beyond my walking into that diner are irrelevant."

Griff refused to believe there was nothing else that
could be done. The sheriff had put in place a road-
block at each end of the boulevard. She'd set up a sort
of command post at Pampered Paws. The view of the
diner from Meg's upstairs apartment provided a good
vantage point. Having all involved come in through
the back had provided decent cover as well.

Norwood continued to argue with Meg's conclusion about what happened next.

Like him, the sheriff believed they needed a damned
better plan for going in.

"Either way," Griff tossed in once more, "I'm going in with you."

Meg looked from Griff to Norwood. "If he goes with me, that's just another casualty to have to deal with, because this will not happen without casualties. The fewer bodies in their path, the fewer lives lost."

Her insistence that Griff couldn't help in any capacity infuriated him. "I'll take that risk," he growled.

Norwood held up a hand for him to settle down. The other four deputies in the room stood back, waiting for orders.

"I've got Deputy Phillips on the second floor of the urgent care. He's got a direct view into the diner. We know this Ridley character has three others with him. Two males, one female. Phillips can take them out if he catches one or more in his crosshairs. He was a sharpshooter in the military. He won't miss."

Meg shook her head. "Ridley will never be that careless, and if one of the others is taken out, there will be retaliation. People will die."

Meg had insisted they call in a bomb squad. Just in case. The one Chattanooga had wouldn't be here for another ten minutes.

"Sheriff."

The word rattled across Norwood's radio. "What've you got, Phillips?"

"Ma'am, look closely at the diner window. Something's happening."

Norwood, Meg and Griff rushed to the window. Norwood had binoculars. Meg had the ones they had found in the cabin. Both peered for a long moment toward the diner. Meg drew back first and passed the pair she'd used to Griff.

He moved closer to the window and set the binoculars in place. Next to him, Norwood swore.

"He's lining them up to provide cover." She swore again.

Jodie, Dottie, Ernie and all the other Piney Woods residents in the diner, including Katie, the owner, now stood in a line along the plate glass window. There would be no sniper shots getting to one of the bad guys. No flash bangs or smoke bombs would be thrown in through the window. Griff drew back. His attention landed on Meg once more.

"I told you he wouldn't take any chances." Meg turned to Norwood. "I'm guessing your man Phillips doesn't have sights on Ridley or any of his people now."

Norwood spoke into the radio. "Phillips, can you get any of the targets in your crosshairs now if they step away from the counter?"

So far, all four had stayed just beyond the sniper's line of vision into the diner.

"Negative," Phillips confirmed.

"It's time," Meg said. "I have to go."

Griff stepped toward her. "I'm going with you." When she would have argued, he said, "Unless Norwood takes me into custody or you kill me, I'm going. Either with you, or I'll run down the middle of the street behind you."

THE MAN WAS the most hardheaded—

Meg drew in a big breath. She was wasting time. "Fine. You can go with me and get yourself killed too."

That was exactly what would happen. They would walk in and they would both be killed. Ridley would likely kill Griff first just to torture her. The endgame was shutting her up. She had nothing else to offer. Nothing to use in trade. The only potential distraction she dared to hope might give her a fighting chance might not come through. At least she had tried.

Norwood pressed her lips together and shook her head in something that resembled defeat. "We've got people in the woods behind the diner. Deputy Porch is working on getting into the diner's attic from the one in the bookshop. If he's successful, he might be able to help. We've got Phillips directly across the street watching through his scope, ready to take one or more out. Roadblocks. Whatever happens, they are not getting away."

Meg decided it was pointless to tell the sheriff that she had no idea who she was dealing with. Ridley would find a way. It wouldn't matter if no one else survived. He would take care of himself above all else. He would vanish like fog rising off a lake in the sunshine.

It was the way they were trained. Meg had her knife in her sock. Her gun at the small of her back. And her one secret weapon that may or may not prove useful.

If she was really, really lucky, it would work, but she'd have to get that extra luck to even hope.

"There's just one more thing," Meg said to Norwood.

"Whatever we can do," the sheriff insisted.

"Get your guy Phillips on the radio."

Norwood did as she asked. "All right."

"Phillips, if you get Ridley in your sights—"

"How will I know which one is Ridley?"

Meg purposely kept her gaze from Griff as she responded, "Because I'll be with him."

Griff's forehead creased in question, but he said nothing.

"Noted," Phillips said.

"If you get Ridley in your sights," Meg went on, "take him out. I don't care if you have to take me out with him. Just take him out."

Meg didn't give Norwood or anyone else time to argue, she walked away. Griff followed. They hurried down the backstairs and out the rear exit of her shop. Griff said nothing, just followed until she had loaded into the SUV.

He stood at the open passenger side door, but he made no move to get inside.

She glared at him. "I have to go."

He nodded. "I know. But don't go to the diner. Drive away. Get as far from here as possible. I'll go take care of this for you."

What the…?

He slammed the door and hurried away. She got out and shouted across the hood. "Griff, we have to go now. Get in the damned vehicle."

He kept going, moving faster. Then he vanished around the corner of the building.

She jumped back into the driver's seat and started the engine. By the time she had backed out and driven around to the street, he was in a dead run and nearly to the diner.

"Son of a…" She rammed the accelerator, barely overtaking him before he reached the diner. She made a hard right and stood on the brake to skid to a stop directly in front of him.

She jumped out and met him at the hood before he could get past her. "Don't even think about it," she warned, the air sawing in and out of her lungs, her heart thundering. She should kick his ass right now.

"You should have kept going," he said, breathless, his voice loaded with something like regret.

The worry, the fear and the hurt in his eyes was like a knife ripping her open. "Just remember one thing for me."

He blinked. "What?"

"If I have to take a call, the moment I say hello, drop like a rock and roll under a table."

"What?"

"Just remember that."

She turned her back on him and walked the remaining few yards to the diner. The terrified faces of her friends and neighbors, as well as Ernie and another deputy, stared out at her as she approached. The fearful gazes sent cracks running clean through her heart. This was her fault.

The one thing that kept her putting one foot in front of the other and not falling to her knees and weeping like a child was the possibility that she would be able to put a bullet in that bastard Ridley's head.

She pushed the door open and walked into the diner. Griff moved up behind her. The bell over the door jangled as it closed.

Besides the people lined up in the window standing on the wide ledge, much like the one in her apartment, there was only Ridley and the female he'd brought with him behind the counter. Meg didn't dare take her eyes off the two to look for the others. They would be here somewhere.

"Only thirty seconds late," Ridley said.

He hadn't changed much. Still wore his jet-black hair military short. Still sported that fashionable stubbled jaw. Tall, handsome, smart. And evil. Her finger itched to wrap around a trigger and put one deep into his skull.

"I'm here, aren't I?" Meg said with a careless shrug.

"Yes, you are."

One of the other two minions appeared from the kitchen. She got it now. They were keeping watch on the rear entrance. It was the only other access to the diner. The third member of this little party patted Griff down, then did the same to Meg. She kept her eyes on Ridley the whole time. He was the one she had to watch. He was the most unpredictable. The one—she knew with complete certainty—who had the most to lose.

Number three took Meg's gun and her knife. She'd known that would happen. Then he took her cell phone. He was new to her. Younger. Blond. Gray eyes. Too bad he'd chosen the wrong side.

He placed all three items on the counter and stepped back, blending into the background near the jukebox to wait for further instructions.

Ridley took aim at Griff. Meg held her breath. "Hope she was worth it, buddy."

Her cell phone rang.

Thank God.

Ridley stared at the phone, then at Meg. "Why is someone calling you?"

Incredibly grateful that his eyes were now on her and not on Griff made her weak in the knees with relief.

"No clue," she lied.

"Answer it," Ridley said to his female cohort. "I know that area code."

The woman stepped forward, picked up the phone and accepted the call. "What?" she barked. Two seconds later, her face paled. Three seconds after that, "Yes, sir," she uttered meekly. She turned to Ridley and extended the phone toward him. "It's for you."

He made a face. "Who the hell is it?"

The woman, her eyes wide, shook her head.

Meg barely restrained a smile. Maybe luck was on her side after all.

Ridley accepted the phone with his left hand and pressed it to his ear. "Who the hell is this?" he demanded with his usual arrogance.

His own eyes flared wide for an instant, then his gaze landed on Meg. She stared right back at him as he listened to the person on the other end of the line.

"She's lying." The weapon in his other hand swung in her direction. "She's freaking lying. You know who is loyal to you."

Fury contorted the features of his face. "One second, sir." He pressed the phone to his shoulder. "Get over here, you damned bitch."

That was her cue. Meg kept her gaze on his as she walked to the other end of the counter and moved behind it. He glared right back at her as she approached him. Gun in his right hand. Phone in his left. She fixed that image in her mind.

He grabbed her around the upper chest with his left arm and jerked her against him. Then he pressed the barrel of his weapon into her temple. She settled her gaze on Griff and urged him with her eyes to stay calm. He looked frantic, terrified. She gave him a wink as if to say, *I've got this*, and his features instantly relaxed.

"Take the goddamned phone and tell him you lied," Ridley roared.

Meg looked up at her former partner, her former colleague, her former lover. The muzzle pressed into her cheekbone. "Who is it?" she asked innocently.

"You know who it is," he snarled. "He suddenly believes I killed his son."

Oh, how she was loving this. The fear and outrage on his face. It was almost worth dying for. But not quite.

"Tell him," he sneered, the muzzle burrowing deeper into her face, "that you lied."

She took the phone from him, pressed it to her ear, her gaze back on Griff. "Hello."

Griff dropped.

The woman stepped forward to peer over the counter. The man at the jukebox moved forward.

Salvadori Lorenzo's voice echoed in her ear. "If you doctored that video somehow," he warned.

Meg braced herself. "I lied…"

The muzzle dug deeper into her temple.

"…it was Ridley—"

She shoved upward on the hand holding the gun.

The weapon fired, barely missing the top of her head.

The phone hit the floor.

Ridley ranted at her, attempting to get a hold on her once more.

The woman drew back from the counter and whirled toward Meg.

In the background, above the screams, she heard Griff shouting for everyone to get down on the floor.

Meg twisted, pulling Ridley with her even as he pulled off another round, this one going over her shoulder, damned close to her ear. Meg twisted again, shoved him backward, but his grip on her was too strong to fall free.

The woman's weapon discharged. The bullet plowed into the side of Ridley's skull. Meg charged the woman, using his suddenly limp body as a barrier between them. She shoved him harder, knocking the woman down. Her weapon discharged again, hitting the wall behind Meg.

Meg dove for the handgun Ridley had dropped. She grabbed it and turned just in time to pull the trigger, sending a bullet between the eyes of the jukebox man who'd jumped over the counter to help his friends.

The sound of the woman scrambling to get out from under Ridley's body had Meg rolling to her left. She pulled off another, hitting the woman in the center of her forehead.

Meg launched to her feet, glancing around. Where was the other guy? Some people were still screaming but all were on face down on the floor. Except…

Where was Griff?

"Drop it."

The warning came from the end of the counter nearest the kitchen door.

Meg turned to the final man, her weapon leveled on him, his leveled on her. "You still have time to run," she suggested.

"No way," he snarled.

She pulled the trigger and sidestepped because she knew he would do the same. The impact of his shot jerked her shoulder.

Another shot blasted in the air.

The man stared down at his chest where blood had started to bloom. Meg looked to her left. Griff stood at the counter, her gun locked in his hands.

The man crumpled to the floor.

Griff had shot him. She apparently missed.

Meg ignored the pain that radiated down her arm as she retrieved the woman's weapon and then the two belonging to the men. That was when she spotted the path a bullet had grazed along the side of the third man's head. So she hadn't missed entirely.

She suddenly became aware of all the crying and shouting around her. Deputy Battles was suddenly at the counter. The other deputy was ushering the people outside.

Griff appeared at her side, ushering her away from the bodies. "An ambulance is on the way. You should sit down."

She glanced at her left shoulder. *Damn.* She'd been hit. On some level she had known it.

Damn.

She looked at Griff then. "You saved my life."

She hadn't even known he could use a handgun, and he'd saved her life.

"Come on," he ushered her from behind the counter and toward a chair.

She glanced around. The place had cleared out in record time. A table to her left had been overturned. An obvious bullet hole marred its shiny red surface.

Her gaze went to Griff. "Are you hit?"

He shook his head as he settled into the seat next to her. "When I hit the floor and rolled under that table, I pulled it down for cover. The only shot the guy got off missed me."

Worry swam through her head, which was also swimming. "You could have been killed."

He grinned. "But I wasn't and neither were you."

She blinked, her eyes stinging. Griff had saved her life.

Chapter Fifteen

Pampered Paws
Pine Boulevard
Friday, May 10, 9:00 a.m.

"You're sure about this?" Jodie said.

Dottie stood next to her, both eyeing Elle with mounting worry.

She smiled. "I am positive."

Jodie turned to Dottie. "Don't get any ideas about taking one of those cruises anytime soon. I can't do this alone."

Elle laughed. She'd turned the shop over to Jodie and given Dottie that bonus she so richly deserved. Both were thrilled. Elle had also turned over her former cover as Megan Lewis to the past. She was back to being her true self, Eleanor Holt, aka Elle. No more being a detective or an undercover agent or a spy. She was just Elle from Piney Woods, Tennessee, who wasn't sure what she intended to do next in terms of a career.

"Meg." Dottie shook her head. "Sorry. Elle, we don't know what to say."

"Don't say anything," she assured her dear friends, "just enjoy."

"You better come see us," Jodie said, her face pinched as if she might cry.

"Don't worry," Elle promised, "I will."

She waved to the two as she walked out the front entrance. She took a deep breath and felt truly free for the first time in years.

In a stunningly brazen move, Salvadori Lorenzo had arrived in Chattanooga early Wednesday morning at the crack of dawn in his private jet. Two of his thugs had shown up at the farm and forced her and Griff into a car. Elle had felt certain that their lives were over. Lorenzo's thugs had taken them to the airfield, where to her shock, Elle had spoken privately with Lorenzo. No matter that the man hadn't deserved her explanation, she told him the truth. She'd spent nearly two years protecting Ridley, and it was time the world knew that she was innocent. Lorenzo's son had discovered that Ridley had been playing both sides of the game—which she had not known at the time— and Ridley had killed him to protect his secret. All this time, Elle had thought she was protecting a fellow agent when Ridley and Wisting had been using both her and Lorenzo for their own selfish gain.

Again, she felt no sympathy whatsoever for Lorenzo. He got as good as he gave. There was an endless list of the people he had betrayed and murdered.

During the brief visit on his personal aircraft, Lorenzo had apologized for sending people to kill Elle and assured her that he would never bother her again. He claimed that though he was a ruthless man, he never ended the life of anyone who didn't deserve to die. With that, he'd left. At the time, Elle had wondered how he would feel when he discovered that in light of what she'd learned from Ridley, her former boss, former Deputy Director Arthur Wisting, had turned State's evidence against Lorenzo. A new multi-agency task force was determined to finally take him down. Hadn't proven relevant in the end, since that very next day after he'd visited Chattanooga, Elle was told that Lorenzo had vanished. With his resources, he could be anywhere in the world.

Nothing Elle could do about that. She had done her part. Her gaze landed on the man waiting for her. She smiled. Griff leaned against the passenger side of his truck.

"You ready?" he called out.

Elle took the two steps down to meet him. "You sure you want to spend an entire week away from the farm?"

"Two of Lonnie's new apprentices have it covered," Griff assured her. "He'll be keeping a close eye on things to ensure all runs smoothly." He opened the truck door. "We are taking a nice, quiet vacation in the middle of nowhere in the vicinity of Gatlinburg. No one," he said pointedly, "knows where we'll be, and I intend to keep it that way."

His mother and sister and numerous neighbors and friends had called and shown up at his door over the past few days. Several ladies with casseroles. Elle had barely kept her laughter to herself when the casse-roles arrived. Basically, his home had been a regular madhouse the past few days. They had decided that a week away was necessary. It would give the story time to drop lower in the news feed and neighbors time to move on to something new to obsess about.

She chewed at her lower lip. "Raymond is going to miss me terribly."

"We'll video-chat with him every day." Griff opened the door for her to get into the truck.

Instead, she moved in next to him. "I'm not sure how much fun I'll be, injured as I am." She glanced at her bandaged shoulder. The bullet had actually missed anything important. Just a flesh wound mostly. Hurt like hell, but she was tougher than she looked.

He leaned down, brushed his lips across hers. "I have every intention of taking very, very good care of you, and then I'm going to bring you back here and show you just how good life can be."

Elle couldn't wait. This man and the life they were going to share on the farm were a dream come true.

She smiled up at him. "What're we waiting for?"

Griff helped her into the truck, and they were off.

* * * * *